THE LAST BURU

More **Strange Matter**™ from
Marty M. Engle & Johnny Ray Barnes, Jr.

THE LAST BURU

Marty M. Engle
Johnny Ray Barnes, Jr.

MONTAGE
BOOKS

Montage Books, a Front Line company,
San Diego, California

ISBN 1-56714-087-4

Printed in the U.S.A.

STRANGE FORCES ™

Rilo the Buru came to the town of Fairfield as a renegade slave, a monster on the run in desperate need of help. He found help in the form of Morgan Taylor and the kids of Fairfield Junior High. Knowing the strength of the forces they were about to face, Rilo performed the ancient Apa Tuni ceremony, bestowing the children with the powers of incredible, supernatural creatures. Now, together they fight to survive in a secret world of terrifying creatures, supernatural treasure-hunting, and paranormal power struggles, while growing ever closer as friends.

To Rilo, they have grown into something more. To him, they are an adopted family, a new tribe to replace the one he lost.

Rilo thought he was the last Buru.

He was wrong.

The strange force known as "Rilo's Runts" have faced the might of the vile Collector when he threatened to destroy their town. They trained in the treacherous Congo where they saved a rare and marvelous animal, the Chipekwe, from the mad hunter Makkal Monard. They encountered and infuriated the supernatural hunters Guerendet and Vicade, preventing a supernatural relic from opening a doorway to a world of monsters, while their town exploded in Halloween media mania.

Now the kids from Fairfield face their greatest challenge, in far-flung locales against overwhelming odds.

And Rilo the Buru must make the hardest decision he has ever had to make.

FAIRFIELD JUNIOR HIGH
ROLL CALL

Morgan Taylor-(appeared in **Strange Matter #7** *Fly the Unfriendly Skies*) Appointed team leader of Rilo's band of adventurers, Morgan thought he was doing a good job. But when his leadership ability is questioned, he's determined to whip his team into shape. Will he go too far, or will he come through when the kids need him the most? **Morgan can transform into a Gargoyle, capable of breathing fire and flight.**

Frank Dunk-(appeared in **Strange Matter #6** *Bad Circuits*) With new additions to his team, Frank has grown very suspicious. He believes the others are letting power get in the way of clear thinking. Will he shed light on new, unseemly forces before the team pays the price? **Frank shifts to the form of a giant snake and spits acidic venom.**

Michelle Boyd-(appeared in: **Strange Matter #5** *The Last One In*) Michelle is completely fed up with the rest of the group. All they seem to care about is completing their goals, without any concern to the innocents caught in their destructive battles. Can she make the others truly see those who pay the price for their recklessness? **Michelle transforms into a large golden Thunderbird.**

Hank Dunk-(appeared in **Strange Matter #6** *Bad Circuits*) Hank's proven himself as a useful member of the group, but he believes his brother Frank still dismisses him. Hank's going to solve that problem once and for all, but will he survive long enough to make sure his brother learns his lesson? **When needed, Hank can (hopefully) turn into a massive, unstoppable Nandi.**

Kyle Banner-(appeared in **Strange Matter #9** *Deadly Delivery*) Battling to re-establish himself as the one and only Fairfield terror, Kyle is in no mood to have commands barked at him by Morgan. Hanging around Morgan and Frank has affected his judgement, and made him think too much before he acts. Will his next act be a solo? **Kyle thrashes his enemies as a colossal apeish Pendek.**

Shelly Miller-(appeared in **Strange Matter #1** *No Substitutions*) Shelly has become the group's positive center. No matter what they face, she's confident they can handle things and come out on top. However, is she willing to risk the lives of innocents to achieve her goal? **Shelly strikes in the form of an ultra fast Phantom Panther.**

Skinny Joe Alister-(appeared in **Strange Matter #11** *Something Rotten*) Around school, Joe's become what he used to fear—a bully. His powers have given him all the confidence he's ever hoped for, and now he wants to enter a dangerous game to prove himself amongst the hunters of the supernatural. But in doing so, is he not only endangering himself, but his team as well? **Skinny Joe turns into a powerful snarling Black-Hound.**

Darren Donaldson-(appeared in **Strange Matter #3** *Driven to Death*) Darren's tired of having his abilities questioned by his friends, especially his older brother. He's going to show them once and for all that he's just as good as he says he is, and that means joining Skinny Joe on his dangerous journey. Will Darren put his money where his mouth is, or will he wind up cashing in? **In an instant, Darren becomes a howling mad Werewolf.**

David Donaldson-(appeared in **Strange Matter #3** *Driven to Death*) David, desiring a normal, high-school life, is still trying to get away from Rilo and the group. His little brother Darren keeps pulling him into their adventures. After a near-fatal encounter, David insists that adventuring is simply too dangerous. But can David actually leave when Darren needs him the most?

Preston Talmalker- (appeared in **Strange Matter #25** *Splitting Image*) With a watchful eye on Fairfield, its supernatural visitors, and its young adventurers, Preston has waited for the perfect time to approach Morgan's group. His chance has finally come. But whose side is he really on?

FAIRFIELD'S CHAMPIONS

Morgan Tayler

The world awakened on time—eight o'clock on that Saturday morning. Murray Peel's bumper scraped the driveway as he left for the golf course. The McAlister's dog was barking its usual morning greeting. The paperboy delivered the Saturday news with a wet slap of rolled print at the door.

But it was still a workday for the rumpled, twelve-year-old Morgan. He sat in front of the active computer screen, his serious, hound-dog face bathed in blue light. He'd been up since five o'clock.

Research was the reason. The night before, he'd begun sorting through his computer files before he went to bed. Anxious to finish, he got up early that morning. Now, munching on a breakfast bar and running his hand through his uncombed hair, he watched the slow progress of the status bar as the computer copied his monstrous load of files to backup storage. Then, between crunchy chews, he heard a faint scratching sound.

And suddenly, *something attacked his window.*

He shifted instantly. Shifted *into his Gargoyle form.*

Morgan's skin pigment changed to gray as his muscles and bone structure stretched and bulged, his body enlarging in a single breath. With his eyes glowing a fiery red and wet, batlike wings folding into ready position, he snarled upon learning the source of the attack.

Claws, the McAlister's cat. The one their dog was always barking at during that time of the morning.

With a sigh of relief, he shifted back to human form, feeling his flesh practically snap back in to position at the the end of the transformation. The miracle of such a change had worn off on him now. In those first few weeks after the ceremony, Morgan had transformed constantly, discovering new awareness, new sensations, and new powers each time he had done so. It was amazing to him that just one simple ceremony could give a human being such abilities. One simple act that, to the best of Morgan's knowledge, was a secret kept from the rest of the world.

But he had to wonder . . .

He pulled up his customized search engine and typed in two words he'd never input before.

APA TUNI.

The program searched. It came up with nothing. Besides what he already knew, which was very little, Morgan had no information on the Apa Tuni tribe of India, whose supernatural ceremony had given Morgan his powers.

Curious, Morgan went on the Web. He went through search after search, coming up with bits and pieces of information about the tribe, but nothing concerning the ceremony.

Then he came across a meager newsgroup posting.

An eyewitness account of the ceremony. The sender was anonymous, but Morgan had ways of finding the source. For now, he simply downloaded the message.

As he watched the gray status bar creep across his screen, he became aware of the frenzied barking of the McAlister's dog. It sounded like it was going mad. Its growls became more vicious. It snarled between yelps.

Morgan felt the hair on the back of his neck rise.

The air behind him crackled.

He spun around in his chair, shifting again into Gargoyle form as a rip appeared in the air, spitting light in all directions. It grew larger and brighter, then suddenly closed in on itself.

Something fell to the floor, striking the hardwood with a crack. The projectile looked to be a cylinder. It stood on end, smoking from the journey.

Morgan got off his chair and waved away the smoke. The tube had metal wrapped around each end and a heavy, clear glass center. There was a twist handle on one end. Morgan cautiously turned it, releasing the vacuum of air inside. He peered through the last wisps of smoke that seeped out and saw a small envelope at the bottom of the cylinder. He removed it and was only mildly surprised that it was addressed to him. Opening it, he read the note as a computerized voice behind him announced that his download was complete.

"Frank?"

"Yes, Hank?"

"Will this fry my head?"

"No, Hank. Just put on the Impositron Helmet, please."

Hank slipped on what looked like a motorcycle helmet with a lawn mower engine attached to the top. The visor that folded over his eyes was ruby red, with one glowing yellow dot appearing in the center.

"Use that yellow dot to focus on a fixed point, then press this button," twelve-year-old Frank explained, handing his younger brother a one-button remote control that was wired to the helmet."

"Wh-What will this do?" stammered Hank, sweat practically pooling in his hands.

"Once you've chosen a spot, push the button. Invisible, Dunk-patented, concentrated rays will fire from the helmet to strike that spot in the air. There will be a flash of light, and a block of ice will fall to the ground. I haven't thought of any practical use for this device yet, but eventually it will help me conquer things. Now, Hank, perform for me," Frank ordered, as he placed a flat, wood-

5

en stick in Hank's mouth for him to bite on.

"Whaff thiff for?" Hank asked.

"Just in case," Frank said.

Hank settled in and narrowed his eyes. He focused on a point in front of him. A nice, friendly looking point.

Suddenly a brilliant light sliced through the space in front of them. Something dropped to the floor, and then the light was gone.

"Brilliant, Hank! You did it!" Frank yelled.

"But I never pressed the button," Hank whined.

Frank's brows furrowed, and he walked over to kick at the smoking cylinder—not a block of ice—that lay on the floor. He looked at his brother, who shrugged at him, completely clueless.

Michelle Boyd

She did this rarely, but sometimes Michelle couldn't help herself.

And why not, she would argue with herself. *What would any other eighth-grader with powers like yours do?*

She had gotten up early that morning and

hiked to Miller's Peak. Now, she stood on the high overlook, peering down the slick rock face to see the faint clouds of mist drift slowly past.

Stretching out her arms and holding them high, she initiated her transformation. It took no more than a thought and an instant of tensing her entire body. Then, she grew warm as her blood seemed to flow faster than before, and her body tingled. She felt as if tiny trees sprouted from her skin as her flesh toughened and feathers emerged from her pores. Michelle's eyes turned milk white, then burned red, as if she were boiling inside. Her breathing always grew shallower when her skull hardened and a beak formed from the petrified flesh over her nose and mouth. Next came the wings, as two large humps formed under the skin on her back, then pushed through with sharp-ended tips. They unfolded, still moist from the transformation, and expanded like a feathered hang glider attached behind her. They waved slightly in the breeze.

As she marveled at the world through this highly sensitive bird-like form, she noticed the steel ring that was driven into the edge of the rock face. She saw the red-and-black rope that was threaded through it, and watched the rope

7

stretch as something pulled on it. Then, from over the edge, she saw a rock climber appear.

He saw her and screamed. Losing his grip on the rope, he fell backward over the edge.

It took Michelle less than a second to soar over the rock face and snatch the plummeting man out of his free fall to the earth.

The rock climber was still screaming as Michelle dropped him down gently on a level area of Miller's Peak. Then, she flew off, rationalizing to herself that if she had been a real monster, the poor man would have surely perished.

As she flew away, wondering how to explain of this incident to Rilo, a light flashed in front of her. She swerved as something dropped out of the light. Catching it in her claws, Michelle could read the envelope inside through the clear container. It was addressed to her.

Kyle Banner

"So, Banner, we meet again," Count Nefarious drawled, his slow-syllabled accent coming across loud and smug.

"What are you three twerps doing?" Kyle

demanded, as the door to the Quicky-Mart closed behind him. The ex-Fairfield Junior High Super-Bully, a grimacing hulk clad in red-and-white flannel, stood in the parking lot slurping his Tyranno-Gulp while staring into the angry faces of the Terrible Trio—Wolf, Blade, and Count Nefarious, his would-be successors in scholastic terrorism.

The three of them surrounded him: Wolf, the short feisty one, whose unwashed curly hair formed a bird-nest tangle on top of his head; Blade, slightly taller, vastly simpler, and grossly pudgy, whose eyes were half covered by his dark blue ski cap; and Count Nefarious, a blond-haired beanpole whose old pinstripe shirt hung down over too-blue, bargain-bin jeans. They circled Kyle's hulking form like nervous hyenas.

"We've come to mess you up, Banner. Mess you up good!" Blade retorted with a snort.

Kyle stayed cool.

"Fellas, you realize your actions, here, completely negates our last meeting don't you?"

The Terrible Trio looked confused.

"Negates? What does that mean?" Wolf snarled.

Kyle suddenly realized that his vocabulary was expanding and attributed it to hanging

9

around eggheads like Frank Dunk.

"It means you didn't get the message the last time we met, did you?" Kyle asked.

"We got your point," Count Nefarious seethed, "but now we have a secret weapon! **Ninja Rick! Attack!**"

Suddenly, from around the side of Quicky-Mart corner came a figure doing flip after flip, spinning toward Kyle like a human wheel. The figure—a kid—landed on his feet just in front of the former bully and struck a classic martial arts pose.

"Hiiiiyaahhh!!!"

The kid wore a black ninja suit and an intense stare.

"Ninja Rick, here, transferred from Mullenfield where he studied under the great ninja master Rama Tao! He's a one-boy weapon with more moves than a room full of ants!" boasted Count Nefarious.

"Hiiiiyaahhh!!!" Ninja Rick yelled again, and struck Kyle's slurpy cup with his fingertips. The cup soared through the air, then smashed on the ground, sending Slushee everywhere.

Kyle shot Ninja Rick a burning red stare, then thrust out a hand, grabbing the karate kid by the shirt and hoisting him into the air. Ninja

Rick let loose with kick after kick, but it had no effect. Finally, he started to whimper.

"Sorry, Ninja Rick!" Wolf yelled, as the Terrible Trio turned tail and ran. "You don't have what it takes to be the fourth member of the Terrible Trio!"

Sweaty and scared, Ninja Rick peered into Kyle's eyes, pleading silently for his future.

"Wh-What is your secret?" Ninja Rick squeaked nervously.

Kyle grinned.

"No secret. I've just got my own kind of magic is all."

As he dropped Ninja Rick and watched him run away, Kyle felt a strong breeze blow up from behind him. He turned in time to see a flash of light and hear something strike the parking lot asphalt. He blinked once and the light was gone. Only a heavy, clear cylinder was left. It rolled to a stop at his feet.

"Good," Kyle muttered, "I was just beginning to get bored."

"So I told the zombie, 'Wow, you look like you've had a rotten day!' Get it? *Rotten* day! Come on, David, that's a laugh riot," Darren said, trying to get his older brother to look up from the hood of his car.

"It's funny, but it's not *HA HA* funny," David replied, growing weary of his twelve-year-old brother's shenanigans. Darren was a short, grinning mop-haired spitfire. David was the taller version, only his face was soured, pulled into an undertaker's frown, as though his fire had been spit on. "Can you hand me that wrench off the ground, please?"

Darren sneered, and then, every bit the dark-haired rascal, shifted his hand to Werewolf mode. He handed his brother the wrench, wrapped in a large, brown-fur-covered claw.

"Rere you ro, Ravid," he growled in his best Scooby Doo voice.

"HEY!" David jumped, banging his head on the open hood. "Cut that stuff out! Mom and Dad might see you!"

"Nah, I'd sense them," Darren replied. "You really ought to have Rilo perform the Apa

Tuni ceremony on you, Bro. Having supernatural powers is a kick."

"I don't think Rilo gave them to you for kicks," David said, adjusting the bolts on his carburetor. "Besides, I wouldn't want them. Since you've gotten those powers, all you seem to do is get into trouble. Maybe you should think about laying off all this crazy treasure hunting for a while."

"Lay off? Why would I do that? It's too much fun! Admit it, David, you have fun when you're with us, don't you?"

Darren waited for an answer, but David stayed silent and continued to work on his car.

"Well . . . don't you?" Darren asked again.

"Yeah," David mumbled halfheartedly. "A blast."

His cynical statement was punctuated by a thunderous crack, as the sunlight behind them suddenly seemed brighter. They spun around in time to catch the light disappearing and saw the silhouette of something drop heavily onto the driveway. As it started rolling down the slope toward the street, Darren went after it, and David sighed, knowing that the craziness was starting early that day.

"Curtis?!" Shelly asked, brushing her blond ponytail off her shoulder. An eighth-grade police girl in search of a case, she anxiously pedaled up to the ditch. She had seen one bicycle wheel sticking out of it, spinning in the air like a wind chaser.

"Yeah, it's me," Curtis Chapman moaned, his whole body stinging from the crash as he climbed out from under his bike. "The Terrible Trio's at it again. They crashed me and snatched my Gameboy and Werewolf Hunter cartridge from my pocket. Then, they took off on their bikes. Man, when I tell—"

"There they go around the corner!" Shelly yelled, pointing to the intersection at the end of the street. In the blink of an eye, she was on her bike, speeding after them.

"Shelly! Don't!" Curtis yelled, but it was too late. Shelly had already turned the corner in pursuit.

Her eyes glowed red as she pedaled after the Trio, who saw her coming and quickly crossed the busy street. Shelly's supernatural reflexes were on high, and she zipped into the street amid

14

oncoming traffic. The drivers swerved and stomped on their brakes to avoid her, and by the time she had crossed the intersection, she had almost caused a six-car pileup.

But Shelly didn't realize it. Her attention was focused on the Terrible Trio as they abandoned their bikes at the edge of the road and disappeared into the woods. Shelly pedaled toward the woods at full speed, and when she reached the edge, she leaped over her handlebars. Her bike fell behind her as she shifted to Phantom Panther form and lunged into the woods. She picked up the Trio's scent as soon as she hit the ground.

The Trio heard something coming after them hard and heavy. They tore through the woods as if they were running for their lives. Then, suddenly, the noise behind them stopped. Moments later, the Trio stopped to catch their breaths.

"Y-You see anything?" Blade asked his compatriots.

"Yeah. Three morons with a stolen Gameboy they don't even know how to turn on," a growling voice came from behind.

They spun around to see the large, fierce golden cat stalking them just a few feet away.

"Drop the Gameboy and the cartridge, and

15

then run like crazy," Shelly the Phantom Panther snarled.

Both items hit the ground a second afterward, and the three menaces scrambled through the woods, out of sight.

Shelly walked over to retrieve Curtis's possessions. Instead of changing back to human form and grabbing them, she decided to scoop them up with her mouth.

She clamped down too hard with her teeth on the cartridge and heard a crunch. No more Werewolf Hunter.

Oh, well . . . she thought, just as a flash of light appeared to her right.

Skinny Joe Alister

The Terrible Trio had run all the way back to their hideout, the Devil's Tower. It was a tree house constructed in one of the tallest trees at the edge of Fairfield's Dark Woods. It was their fortress. It was impenetrable.

As they climbed to the top, they found someone sitting inside, waiting for them.

"Skinny Joe Alister!" Count Nefarious

yelled, his head being the first to poke up into the stronghold. "You must have a death wish!"

"Come on in, guys," Skinny Joe said in a low voice. He was curled into a ball in the corner, his head resting on his pale, thin arms. His straight brown hair hung down over his eyebrows, framing his unflinching stare. "I've been waiting for you."

"Yeah? Some guys wait for weeks for one of our behind-kickings," Wolf said, climbing in behind Nefarious. Blade came in last, too stunned at Joe's nerve to say a word. His jaw simply dropped.

"I'm not here for a behind-kicking," Skinny Joe replied. "I'm here to deliver the news."

"What news? Did you gain some weight?" Count Nefarious snorted, jabbing Wolf with his elbow as a signal to join in the snorting.

"No," said Skinny Joe. "It seems you've started extorting lunch money again, and last week, you shook down my little brother, Gary, for his. That's not going to happen again."

"Oh, yeah?" Count Nefarious bucked up, as the three bullies moved toward Skinny Joe, who rose to meet them. His scarecrow body moved with eerie certainty. Standing upright in front of them, he was ready.

"Yeah. See, that's the news," Skinny Joe snarled, grabbing Count Nefarious's shirt in one lightning-fast move. Wolf and Blade had no time to react, standing dazed as beanpole grabbed beanpole. Skinny Joe pushed Nefarious back through the entry hole, letting him hang in the air. Terrified, Count Nefarious looked at the ground, then peered back up at Joe with pleading eyes. Skinny Joe's own eyes were glowing red.

"I'm not the punk Skinny Joe you once knew. Things are different now, and if you ever bother me, my brother, or any of my friends again, you're going to have to learn how to fly! Got it, Count Nerferter?"

Count Nefarious whimpered through his tears and nodded. Skinny Joe pulled him back up and tossed him to the floor, then looked at Blade and Wolf, who were not about to mess with him.

Skinny Joe smiled, then made his way back down the ladder. He didn't quite make it out of the woods before the rip appeared.

The morning shone down upon the isolated majesty of Fairchild Manor. Sitting on its historic spot just outside Fairfield, the old-world style mansion had inspired many stories over the years. Lately, it had even been the selected spot for a massive gathering of freaks, party-goers, and reporters. But now, the hype had faded. There were too many other anomalies in town garnering attention, and this grand piece of history had already received its moment in the sun.

And that made its present resident, Rilo Buru, very happy.

Every day there were fewer people coming over the front iron gate, tiptoeing through the cemetery, and climbing the concrete stairs to reach the sleeping giant of a home. There weren't as many people knocking on the thick wooden door, peering in through its antique glass window, or twisting the knob and trying to enter. Yes, these annoying disturbances were slowly decreasing.

Which gave Rilo time to redecorate a little.

As he hung the last picture, the four-foot-high, scaly green creature known as Rilo Buru put the final touch on the family room.

At least, it used to be the family room. The Buru could not imagine Langdon or Anastasius Fairchild, one-time owners of Fairchild Manor—now Rilo's home—ever having had the kind of family that called for a family room. But that's the purpose it must have served. Family pictures had hung in the room when Rilo first arrived. Many of them had been damaged in the great Halloween Battle at Fairchild Manor, so Rilo decided to give them a rest. He had taken the remainder down, and in their place hung his own family pictures.

Morgan, Frank, Hank, Michelle, Kyle, Darren, David, Shelly, and Skinny Joe—Rilo's Fairfield family. He decided this room would now be a room of honor. The Hall of Heroes, though he wouldn't tell the kids that. Some of them were already getting big heads. No, he'd keep that to himself. Besides, they already knew he was proud of them.

Of course, they weren't his real family. Rilo had the distinction of being the last of the Buru. The rest of his kind had been attacked in the night and destroyed by the Collector. Rilo, however, was kept alive. He believed it was because of his unique rapport with humans and his knowledge of the human mind. In that way, Rilo had always stood out from his Buru brethren. He had a curiosity about humanity that the rest of his species had lacked. How the Collector had known that about him he would probably never know.

He did know that he missed his old life, but the void was filled somewhat by his new friends in Fairfield. He was their leader. The sage who had saved them from the evil Collector's invasion and had given them supernatural powers to defend themselves against the unspeakable horrors they'd faced.

Never once had they looked at Rilo in the way he thought of himself.

A failure.

He felt this at the very core of his being. He had failed the Buru. If he was so special, if he was truly the gifted one of his species, shouldn't he have found some way to save his comrades? His real family?

This was the guilt he lived with daily, ever since he'd been captured and even after he'd escaped. In his most private moments, he asked himself, out of all of the Buru, why had the fates chosen him to live? Why was Rilo the last Buru?

Suddenly, a light flashed in the den, the glow spilling through the family room doorway.

Rilo crouched and crept toward the opening, ready for an ambush. He moved to the edge of the doorway and peered through, just in time to see a shimmering opening, appear in midair and release something heavy onto the floor. Rilo stayed put until he saw the dimensional door shrink and disappear as quickly as it had come.

Rilo moved over to the object, instantly recognizing what he saw.

"It was only a matter of time," Rilo muttered, as he twisted the end open and pulled out the envelope inside. He quickly tore it open and read:

THE TIME HAS COME FOR ANOTHER HUNT. YOUR PRESENCE IS REQUESTED AT THE SALEM QUEEN.

"The Salem Queen . . ." Rilo sighed, remembering the last gathering he had attended there. A knock on the door interrupted his thoughts.

"Not thrill seekers," he groaned. Even though the disturbances had decreased, there were still those kids who were convinced that Fairchild Manor was haunted. And Rilo had to pay for their curiosity.

He quietly tip-clawed to the door while rereading the note. As always, he planned to whip the door open and scare the color from the kid's hair. It was his only defense against keeping his home from being invaded by them.

So when he turned the knob and thrust his hissing head outside the door, he was astounded to see that his visitor wasn't a kid . . .

But another Buru.

"Uh, hi," the familiar, dark brown, tiger-striped creature growled uneasily.

Rilo, unable to say anything, felt his knees go weak and his balance teeter. He fell forward in a shocked faint.

ROUNDING UP THE HUNTERS

Guerendet

The sign on the glass read V. M. Guerendet, Collector of Antiquities. Housed in an old magic warehouse, Guerendet leased the entire structure, which allowed him to keep it as messy as he wanted.

Inside his office, boxes were stacked in every corner, with mail tubes and envelopes scattered on the floor. The objects that would eventually be contained inside these packages were also spread haphazardly around the room. A rare shrunken head lay beside the trash can. Old stone tablets were stacked next to the filing cabinets. A clear box of ancient metallic scrap sat on the floor near the desk.

Guerendet, a corpulent creature of pale

blue skin, cue-ball eyes, and a horned hairstyle, waddled into the chaotic mess, his brows lifting slightly as he noticed the newest piece of clutter.

"SNOD! JERRY! What is this thing on my desk?" the owl-like megalomaniac shouted as he sat down to go over the day's business.

Jerry—young, thin, smiling, twenty-something—crept into the room, followed by the walking mound of blubbering pus that was called Snod.

"Oh, hey, Big G, that came through a rip in time and space for you this morning! I would have given it to you then, but you were, ahem, indisposed," Jerry chuckled. Snod gurgled in agreement.

Guerendet gave them both the evil eye.

"Hmm. Well, it's a good thing! Never interrupt me when I'm singing a show tune. Ever. So what is this thing, an invitation to Vicade's birthday party? Are we gonna get to wear the cone hats?"

Jerry chuckled again at the whimsical genius that was his boss.

"No such luck, Big G. It looks like you've been invited to a contest by some mysterious yet compelling Game Master."

Snod gurgled.

Guerendet looked over the invitation suspiciously.

"Did you check this for runes, spells, or other written curses?" he asked.

"It's clean, Big G. Just a simple invitation to what is probably one complicated problem," Jerry snorted.

"Well," Guerendet grinned. "This Game Master's problems are just beginning, cause we're going to his party! Break out the noisemakers!"

Jerry laughed.

Snod pulled out an actual noisemaker and started spinning it around.

The laughter stopped, all eyes on Snod.

Vicade

"We've searched the entire apartment, sir. The items are not here. And we found no one hiding," the pale woman said in a monotone voice. Whatever emotion she felt was hidden behind her mirrored sunglasses.

Her employer was dressed all in black, a mountain of tough red skin wrapped around a tremendous physique. He clenched a gigantic fist upon hearing the news. As four other females, identical to the one who had spoken, ransacked the rest of the dwelling, he turned to a trembling, scruffy young man who was tied to the only chair in the room that remained upright.

"My name is Vicade. Has your roommate, Norman, ever mentioned me?" the crimson giant asked.

The young man, who was also wearing sunglasses as well as large logoed K-FNG black T-shirt, shook his head fervently.

"No, man. Normey doesn't tell me much! We're from different worlds! I'm a deejay! He's an accountant! I don't even know what we're doing, living together! He doesn't even pay for his half of the groceries! "

Vicade got into the boy's face. His piercing, emerald eyes leered at his own hideous reflection in the young man's lenses.

"Listen, Deejay, your roommate intercepted some valuable information from me. And since he doesn't seem to be anywhere around, my guess is that he ran with it. That information will take him to something very rare that I desperately want. So tell me, Deejay, where do you think he went?"

"He better not have gone anywhere!" the deejay exclaimed. "Rent's due tomorrow, and he hasn't given me a check!"

Vicade rolled his eyes and caught a glimpse of a tower of old vinyl records in the corner. With a wry grin, he casually walked over to them.

"Tell me," Vicade asked, "are these yours?"

"Oh, yeah," the deejay grinned. "That's my pride and joy. I've never been able to get into CDs, you know. The vinyl just sounds so natural. So organic. You can flip through them if you want. I've got Wasp, Deep Purple, Dexy's Midnight Runners, Lou Rawls . . ."

"I'm going to burn them if you don't tell me where Norman the Accountant is," Vicade told him.

"What? No, man, no! My collection's a peaceful collection! It would never—"

"Do you want me to burn something else? Something of Norman's? Tell me where he is!

The deejay looked at his feet.

"The Serengeti. Norman's in the Serengeti," he sighed.

"Thank you," Vicade smiled, then took a deep breath. His neck bulged to the size of a basketball as he turned to the record collection and spit a burst of flame. The vinyl tower caught fire instantly.

"NO!" The deejay cried, his glasses falling to the floor and tears running from his red eyes.

"You are far too nostalgic," Vicade

announced, as a burst of light erupted behind him. He spun around, assuming a battle-ready position, as his employees moved in to help. They watched a sparkling light deposit a clear cylinder on the floor, then disappear.

Vicade's number one employee grabbed it quickly. Pulling a device from her coat, she waved it over the container.

"It's clean," she said, and Vicade nodded back to her as the vinyl inferno roared behind them and the deejay's wails filled the room. She pulled out an envelope out of the cylinder and handed it to her employer.

"Well," Vicade said as he read it, "it looks as if our plans for the day are detouring. Let us take our leave. We have business elsewhere."

As Vicade and his group left the apart-ment, the deejay, spurred by mental anguish, broke his bonds and jumped out of the chair. He tried futilely to slap out the flames with his leather jacket, but the records continued to burn. His heart broken, he ran to the door and screamed bloody vengeance.

Rising early that morning, Amali had been first to notice the artifacts and the sealed box that contained them were gone. Transformed by anger, her eyes, normally black, had glowed red, and her chalk-white skin had become white-scaled.

"I should have never trusted Norman. Just because he helped us acquire a few other pieces was no reason to count on him extensively," Amali said, as she, her father, and their Werejaguar enclave moved cautiously through the tall Serengeti grass.

"It's not your fault," Rem Tullock comforted her. "He's human."

Amali brushed her long black hair away from her eyes and gazed at her father, the epitome of nobility. He was tall, his long silver hair blowing under his wide-rimmed white hat in the African wind. He wore a light-colored cloak that protected his pale skin from the daylight. But every so often, he'd peer up at the sky, the sun reflecting off the silver marble that had replaced his right eye. A gentleman in the wilderness, tracking his prize.

"He's also close," Rem said, pointing to a

large tree across the plain.

Amali nodded and signaled the Werejaguars to surround the tree. The creatures moved in, and when they reached their destination, Amali produced a small crossbow and aimed it at the tree.

"Come out, Norman," Rem commanded. "The hunt is over, and you've got hungry Werejaguars all around you. Your only chance is to show yourself, and we may be merciful."

From behind the large tree, a trembling, pale man in a business suit stepped into view, sobbing and shaking his head.

"Please, Mr. Tullock, I'm sorry," he whimpered.

"Whom did you give it to, Norman? Remember? The clear box filled with those fragments we've been searching for for a month? When you stole it that night, whom did you meet and give it to?" Rem asked eloquently, his brow slightly furrowing over his silver eye.

Norman looked at the Werejaguars stalking him on all sides and at Amali, who had him in the sights of her crossbow.

"G-Guerendet. I gave it to some guys who worked for Guerendet," Norman squeaked.

"And they double-crossed you, leaving you

here to be hunted by us," Rem deduced. "You certainly know the art of the deal, Norman. Well, I'm afraid I can't let this act go unpunished. After the Werejaguars are finished with you, I'll let my daughter put you out of your misery."

He signaled his team of creatures to move in just as the air beside the tree sliced apart, its hue blending oddly with the bright sunlight.

Seeing his last chance to live, Norman dived through the rip just as something fell out and rolled on the ground until it came to rest at Rem Tullock's feet.

"He's gone," Amali said angrily, as her father reached for the cylinder on the ground.

"If this came from where I believe it did, he may wish he had stayed here with us," Rem said, as he read the golden invitation.

Anastasius Fairchild, the Collector

He had been staring at the invitation for over an hour. He held it between his two reptilian fingers, his yellow eyes reading the words over and over. The large dark figure, in his dark gray hunting fatigues and pith helmet, understood the words, but he wanted the message to say more. He arched his green reptilian brow, rubbed his fingers over the bone spikes that protruded from his forehead, and mentally commanded the invitation to give him a good reason for attending this "contest."

He wanted it to tear him away from this dig, where he had been for the last two weeks. The dig was one of the largest he'd ever committed his forces to undertake.

He watched the Barghests lead the Pendeks in the massive unearthing. The stone faces of ancient, little-known conquerors stared up at him from their soil prisons, as if curious about their fates.

The Collector pondered. Twice in the last year he had traveled to Fairfield to acquire objects of ultimate power. Twice, he'd had those objects in his grasp. Twice, he'd failed to hold on to them. The children, the Buru's inexperienced soldiers, had foiled his attempts to capture and exploit the supernatural mysteries just beyond the known world. His last great barrier, he had grown fond of calling it. As each day passed, he grew more and more certain that he would never see the other side. Fate seemed to be mocking him.

And that is why he was digging.

He, Anastasius Fairchild, had killed his own brother. He knew that now. And in knowing that he, the Collector, had severed all physical ties with his humanity.

He was a true monster now. Possibly the greatest of his kind, and the most powerful.

What did fate have in store for such a creature?

He looked again at the card.

Perhaps it would be best to go.

Preston Talmalker

His father's study doors had been closed since he left on his trip to Fairfield. After the ever-increasing number of supernatural stories began circulating about the town, Preston had known it would only be a matter of time before his father went there to investigate the sightings. His father was a cryptozoologist, meaning that Preston lived in a world most kids only have nightmares about.

Except Preston liked nightmares.

He liked them so much that he had planted a listening device in his father's study. And on the very day his father booked the rental car to drive into Fairfield, the battery on that listening device died.

So now was Preston's chance to put a new one in. He stood outside his father's large study doors, which were locked tight until the man of the house returned.

The average-size twelve-year-old, whose unusually thick eyebrows set atop skin with a odd green cast, wasn't the most popular in school, and he liked it that way. Hours that would have been spent on useless socializing were instead spent training for situations like this one. Using only a single paper clip, Preston picked the lock to his father's study and entered the cold room.

It was always hard to just walk in without making stops at the various displays on the way to his father's desk. In the corner, the supposed scalp of a Tibetan Yeti was encased in glass. On the shelves were small wooden skeleton replica of reported sea monsters and giant winged creatures. On the walls, articles on important finds his father had either been involved with or admired greatly were displayed in glass frames. Preston had seen the displays many times before, but they never ceased to fuel his imagination. He always got the best ideas after seeing those things.

He walked to the desk and reached under it, feeling around for the tiny receiver he'd taped there so many months before. Unable to grab it, he crawled under the desk, and that's when he heard the crackling.

Preston suddenly felt the air rush around him, and he heard something sparking just in front of the desk. He climbed out from under it in time to see a giant formation of light, shining in the air as if it were passing through a hole in some unseen mirror. In short, there appeared to be a rip in the room's reality. Then, without warning, something dropped from that rip and hit the floor.

Before Preston could move, the light vanished, the air in the room settled instantly. Cautiously, he stepped from behind the desk to see a smoking glass cylinder embedded in the hardwood floor of his father's study. Without thinking, as if uncontrollably drawn to it, Preston grabbed the top of it and twisted it open. He was shocked to find an envelope addressed to his father inside.

Preston ripped it open, read it, and smiled. He had been waiting for this. However, he had no idea it would happen so fast. It was a good thing he was prepared.

His previous mission forgotten, he took

the cylinder and the note and ran out of the study. He stormed up the stairs of the Talmalker mansion and rushed to his room.

There was someone he had to contact.

His ex-friend, Alan Layne, had moved to Fairfield not long ago, but since he and Alan had had quite a "falling out," Preston could not talk to him about all of the fantastic things happening in that town. So when Preston began his own investigation, he decided to keep his inquiries about Fairfield a secret for as long as he could.

That would end now.

He had researched Fairfield in detail. He had read the clippings, watched the news footage, even collected gossip through his many contacts. One name kept popping up.

Morgan Taylor.

And once he had started investigating Morgan, things really began to get interesting. Preston had quickly formulated his plan and waited for the exact moment to set it in motion. Then that cylinder, containing the invitation, had materialized in his father's study, and Preston realized the time had come.

He went to his computer, and typed an e-mail message to Morgan Taylor.

OLD FRIENDS

Rilo dreamt. He dreamed of clear days in India when he and his friend, Norbu, hunted game together in the valleys. He saw them playing tricks on the hunters who came to the valley, searching for the mysterious and legendary Buru. He remembered leaving his friend at the Buru village on the nights that he would watch the Apa Tuni from the trees.

Then, his dream turned dark. He saw the black cloud move in over the valley. He saw the Apa Tuni village be attacked by unspeakably horrible creatures. He saw himself racing back to his village, where his own tribe was also under attack. Then, he saw a net getting thrown over him, and as he fell to the ground, he saw Norbu across the way, netted the same as he. Then something struck Rilo's head, and the dream faded to black.

Out of the blackness, Rilo saw something shimmering in the distance. Rilo seemed to move closer, and the shimmering lights took on a recognizable shape.

A city. A glimmering vermilion city with tremendous structures jutting upward to the heavens. A large bridge led into the gates of the shimmering metropolis, and Rilo saw movement on the bridge. It was a massive crowd of beings running out of the city to greet him at the grand entrance.

Buru. Hundreds of Buru.

Rilo awoke with difficulty. The dream faded from his thoughts as he struggled to open his eyes. Something seemed to be blocking the light. A dark shape loomed above him. Rilo tried to focus on the shape; its features seemed to mirror his own. Its head resembled his own, but flatter, more brown than green, with tiger stripes. Its red eyes seemed wider. As the image became clearer, he could make out a grin on the other's face. Suddenly, Rilo's senses came back to him. He realized he wasn't looking into a mirror. He was lying on the couch in the den, and another Buru was staring him in the face. A familiar one.

"N-Norbu?" Rilo asked in a weak voice.

"<Hello, Rilo,>" the other Buru answered in the short-syllabled, native Buru tongue.

Rilo shot up as if it were the first day of school and he was late. He remembered fainting, so the Buru must have moved him to the couch. His chest was heaving as his eyes took in the full spectacle of a friend who had come back from the dead.

"Y-You were killed!" Rilo gasped, trying to catch his breath. "You and the whole village were killed!"

Norbu backed away a little, uneasy with his old friend now, and uncomfortable in these strange surroundings.

"<We lived,>" he said.

"<What's going on?!>" Rilo cried, jumping to his feet and shifting to his native language. "<Tell me what happened! How did you escape?!>"

Norbu's expression was grim, his voice flat.

"<We didn't escape. None of us did, except you. The rest of us were sold to the highest bidder,>" he said, then stopped speaking in Buru. *"We are enslaved. We are in danger of annihilation. We need your help."*

Rilo felt as if a knife had pierced his heart. He remembered his own enslavement under the

Collector. He remembered barely escaping with his life, believing he was the only Buru that was left. The last Buru.

"Of course, I'll help! I can't believe you've all been alive the whole time. How? How could I not have known?" he asked, reverting to his adopted language as Norbu climbed over the furniture, too nervous to remain still.

"We have been kept hidden. The Collector sold us to a treasure digger named Orin Surr."

Rilo watched Norbu climb onto the couch's seat cushion, then looked out the window to notice the sun's position. He hadn't been unconscious long. It was still mid-morning.

Then, Norbu accidentally stepped on the remote control for the television. He hit the power switch, and MTV's *The Grind* flashed on the screen. Music bellowed through the speakers. He leaped up on the back of the couch, his mouth opening in astonishment.

"It's no problem! I've got it! I've got it!" Rilo yelled over the hip-hop, grabbing the remote and flipping the set off. "Norbu, how did you escape?"

"I tunneled out of the stronghold he keeps us in, then stowed away on the local transport."

"How did you find me?" Rilo asked.

Norbu, growing weary of balancing on the couch, jumped to the floor and nervously roamed some more. He crept into the family room and began studying the pictures on the wall. As he gazed at the young human faces, he answered Rilo's question.

"When I got out, I just ran. I didn't know where to go. We, all of us Buru, thought you were dead, Rilo." Norbu said, as Rilo entered the room behind him. "But then, one night while I crept through one of the modern villages, I saw one of those same picture boxes you have. And I saw your face on the screen. The speaker said the footage was from some kind of Halloween fiasco in Fairfield. When I found out where the town was, I made my way here by hiding in a few cargo holds. I prayed you were still here. You have to help me save our tribe, Rilo."

A stone formed in Rilo's throat as he watched his oldest friend examine the pictures of his new "tribe."

"Of course I will," Rilo answered, almost whispering. "I thought all of you were dead. If I'd known otherwise, I would've scoured the earth to—"

"Don't torture yourself, Rilo. We know there are priorities. We could not expect you to give up valuable time to search for us. You or your new friends. Are these them?" Norbu asked, motioning to the pictures.

"Yes," Rilo answered, even softer.

"Heh, Rilo's Runts," Norbu chuckled.

"What?!" Rilo asked in surprise.

Norbu looked at him, embarrassed.

"I am sorry. That is what everyone calls them. Rilo's Runts. Needless to say, there are some who still do not take you seriously, present company excluded, of course," Norbu said, looking back to the picture wall. He noticed one photograph mysteriously absent. "Rilo, where is your picture?"

"I don't think I'm ready to see my face on any walls yet," Rilo said, then asked, "Norbu, do you have a plan to get them out? Where are they?"

"Located within some of the darkest jungle you will ever see. Orin has us caged in his stronghold. It is awful, Rilo. When we are not working, scientists perform all kinds of experiments on us. I pulled my own specimen tag out of my ear," Norbu said, pointing to a missing chunk of his long ear. Then, he unfolded his claw, which held the bent orange plastic tag. Rilo boiled with anger as Norbu continued. "And no, I do not have a plan. I was hoping you could help me with that."

43

"I will," Rilo said, trying to control his temper. He focused on Norbu's face, still amazed that he was looking at his best friend whom he had thought long dead. "Norbu, it's good to see you."

"You, too, my friend. I'm remembering so much. You and I, the mighty hunters—" Norbu growled, just as the front door opened.

Footsteps traveled from the foyer into the den, stopped for a moment, then came toward the family room.

"Hey, Rilo, we've got trouble," Morgan said as he stepped into the family room. He saw Rilo, then saw his Buru counterpart by the wall. "WHAT THE—! RILO?!"

The shock of what he saw made Morgan slam back against the wall, shifting to full Gargoyle form. Norbu crouched and hissed a warning.

"Relax, Morgan!" Rilo said to him, "This is Norbu, my oldest friend, and he's brought me news. The Buru are still alive."

Morgan's heart continued to race as he heard Rilo's words and saw his eyes light up as he spoke them. Morgan sucked in a little air, trying to comprehend what he'd just been told.

"This . . ." Morgan gasped, his eyes on the second Buru, "this changes everything."

MEETING THE FAMILY

Morgan had recovered from the shock by the time the other kids began to pour in one after the other. As they arrived, the kids first freaked over the sight of another Buru at Fairchild Manor, then went on to describe the invitations they had received so mysteriously through a rip in the atmosphere.

As they gathered in the den, Rilo examined Morgan's invitation and came to a decision rather quickly.

"No one's going to go to this," he said, dropping the card on his fine polished coffee table. "I've heard of this kind of thing. All of these treasure seekers get together and have themselves a contest. The Big Hunt, they call it. One big hunt where only one of them comes out the winner. It's a dangerous game, and those guys play for keeps.

The Collector participated in one while I was in his camp. He went in facing fifty powerful adversaries, and in the end, only he and Rem Tullock walked away alive. We'd be slaughtered."

"Slaughtered?" yelled Joe from the couch. "How can you say that? We've kicked the Collector's butt twice! We trounced Makkal Monard, and we made Vicade and Guerendet look like goofballs!"

"Joe, we've never beat the Collector," Morgan interrupted. "If anything, we've always barely managed to escape with our lives! We're talking about going up against a whole army of Collectors!"

"Big deal!" Darren argued, "We've taken on everything those guys have thrown at us, and we've always throttled it! They've got nothing that can hurt us!"

"Darren, have you forgotten where that thinking got you in our skirmish in Langdon Fairchild's lab?" Rilo asked, growing slightly angry. "You practically bled to death after that other Werewolf carved you up! This isn't going to be just a Werewolf, this is going to be warfare!"

"Rilo's right," Michelle said, cautiously eyeing Norbu as he lingered behind the couch, "there are better things we can do with our time. We don't always have to be out there grabbing treasures and showing the other hunters what a good team we are."

Shelly snorted with laughter as she leaned back on the couch. Norbu's claw reached from behind and flicked her ponytail, as if to see if it were alive.

"What do you want us to do?" Shelly asked, "use our powers to plant more trees?"

Norbu emerged from behind the furniture and sniffed around the kids. He sensed before anyone that Michelle wasn't amused.

"You know, at least it would be better than cruising blindly on your bike into oncoming traffic! My mom said she almost hit you and that you practically caused a pileup!"

"I was delivering my hometown from the scourge of evil, and justice doesn't stop for traffic lights!" Shelly snapped back.

"Hey, guys, don't fight!" Hank yelled, standing up from his seat on the floor. Norbu crept toward him and poked him in the belly with his claw. Hank giggled. Norbu felt the boy's arm, amazed at how soft and weak the flesh was. He wondered why Rilo would team with such a fragile species.

"This is ridiculous," David said, throwing up his arms and edging closer to the door. "These meetings are getting more and more out of hand."

His desire to quit was obvious to the others, but no one said anything. Not for the next few seconds. Frank remained unusually quiet, his eyes never leaving Norbu.

Kyle simply slouched in the corner, unwilling to participate in the squabbling. His mind was already made up. If there was a big fight going on, he wanted to be there.

Finally, Morgan broke the silence.

"Well, listen. If Rilo says we shouldn't take this bait, I agree with him. Besides, none of us know exactly where the invitations came from. It could be a trap."

"Besides," Frank finally spoke, his eyes still on Norbu, "I believe priority has been set by the arrival of Rilo's friend, here."

"My name is Norbu, human," the Buru said, disdain apparent in his voice.

Before Frank could reply, Rilo said to the others, "Frank is right. Norbu has escaped from captivity and come to us for help. He says the other Buru are alive and enslaved. They're being kept in a research facility somewhere in the deepest jungles of Africa, and they're being experimented on. I feel it's my responsibility to try to save them, and I hope that the rest of you will accompany me."

"WHAT?" Norbu scoffed, "you are their leader! Order them to come with you, Rilo! If this is your tribe, it is their duty!"

Rilo was stunned.

"I-I don't work that way. Everyone here has a choice," he said.

"Hmmph," grunted Norbu. "What kind of command is that? You have to rule them completely! Who else do you think is going to properly lead this group? Him?" he asked, pointing scornfully at an outraged Morgan. Norbu didn't hesitate as he leaned toward Rilo and warned, "This is not going to be a children's game! If you lead infants into this, you'll lose! The Buru are a proud tribe, Rilo! We would not be captive if this man was not extremely powerful!"

"I've always helped lead this team, and we've always come through these situations alive!" Morgan exclaimed furiously, unable to contain himself any longer. "Who are you to judge us?"

Rilo was torn, embarrassed by his group's lack of professionalism and angered by his old friend's questioning of his leadership.

"My team is ready for anything," Rilo said stiffly.

"Except the Big Hunt," Kyle announced solemnly.

Joe sat up, nodding hard, as if finally justified.

"Yeah, except the Big Hunt! That really bites, Rilo!"

"Joe, stifle it," Morgan ordered.

"What?" Skinny Joe asked, his brows raised in surprised.

"I said stifle it. I can't believe you guys! After everything Rilo's done for us, you want to go off to some stupid contest and leave his people captives? This is the most important thing in his life, and we're the ones who can help him! We're not going to any Big Hunt, and that's it. I'm team leader, and it's my decision," Morgan answered.

Skinny Joe's eyes glowed red. Darren grabbed Joe's shoulder and tried to reason with Morgan.

"Morgan, you know we always listen to you, but—"

"But nothing. We're not going to the Big Hunt. We're going to help Rilo save the rest of the Buru," Morgan told him, his eyes passing from Darren and Joe over to Norbu. "Rilo, what's the plan?"

Rilo, slightly taken aback by Morgan's sudden show of authority, quickly reviewed what he and Norbu had discussed.

"We're going to leave tomorrow morning, and hopefully be back here before dinner," he began, then Norbu interrupted.

"How is that possible?" the gruff Buru asked. "It took me weeks to —"

"We have a device," Rilo answered. "A metal sliver from an artifact called the Ceques. It is a map to all things supernatural, and it will transport us to whatever spot we wish to go by opening an interdimensional rip in reality."

"Amazing," Norbu answered. "<That beats taking a melgroo.>"

Rilo snickered.

The kids looked on uncomfortably as their Buru friend continued the conversation with Norbu in a language they didn't understand.

A GATHERING AT THE SALEM QUEEN

A rusted old Ford hurtled through the slush and gravel, a surprisingly reckless maneuver, since the back road was not traveled nearly enough to be considered safe. The automobile drove up to the forgotten lounge club, kicking up snow deposited by the storm two nights before, and on up to the cracked cement entrance just under the faded wooden sign that hung over the door.

The Salem Queen.

Demira, its owner for the last seventy years, peeked out the window, curious as to whom would blast by on such a day. *On today, of all days.* She wore a round black hat, with a veil that hung over her eyes. Only her lower face could be seen, her skin almost ice blue in tone. Her gloved fingers tightened around the curtain when she saw who it was. Her hired help for the last ten years, Haney McIntyre, slid the car into his usual parking space beside the lounge, hopped out, and slipped on the snow. Getting to his feet, he rushed inside, apologizing as he opened the door.

"I am sorry, Ms. Demira. I apologize, I really do! Me and the boy did a little ice fishing this morning, and the time just got away from us!" he cried, his dip tobacco still in his mouth. His boss stood just beside the door, waiting for him to get ready. Haney noticed that besides the black hat and gloves, she wore a long black dress. Ms. Demira looked like she was in mourning rather than playing hostess.

"Of all the days, Haney," Demira said, crossing her arms and glaring at the bumpkin as he threw off his jacket and wrestled his apron off the wall hook. "I'm afraid your son will receive a fever for this, and your pay will be docked for today. Don't wear the apron. I have a uniform for you in that box on the table.

Haney grabbed the box, wincing at what awaited him.

"Please Ms. Demira, the boy's still shaking off that malaria you gave him last spring. I won't be late again. I promise—"

"It's either a fever, or his nose bleeds heavily all day. Your choice," she said. Beneath her veil, her mouth curved in a smile.

Haney sighed, and chose the punishment for his son.

"A fever it is, then Ms. Demira. Is everyone downstairs?"

"Downstairs and waiting for service," she told him as she walked off.

Haney sighed again and got into uniform.

Tugging at his sleeves, Haney stepped into the elevator that was located in the back of kitchen. He pushed the bottom floor button and continued to adjust his outfit. He looked like a bell boy, only his suit was black, a morbid match for his employer.

The elevator doors opened and a thick mist drifted in. Haney stepped out of the door into a room that was as noisy as it was cloudy. At first, he struggled to see through the smoke, and when he did, stood face to face with a large, bubbling, pus-headed creature.

"Why, Mr. Snod! How're you doin'? Can I get ya anything?" Haney smiled, remembering the lovely Christmas card he had received from

Guerendet's big bruiser last year.

Snod's green eyes bulged slightly, and his mouth opened, emitting a deep, dripping, salutary gurgle. The gelatinous giant held his glass of milk up to toast his favorite servant and accidentally squeezed. The glass exploded, and Haney closed his eyes, letting the tiny shards zoom past as if it happened all the time. Suddenly, Jerry poked his head between the two of them.

"Hey, guys—what's happening here? Hey, Haneymeister! Guess what, guy? My glass, here, is all the way empty. And Snoderico's milk glass is everywhere. The Snodfather requires that thick chalky beverage to keep his mucas running properly! And me, I'm just nutty about the sparkling taste of Fresca."

"I'd be delighted," Haney answered, taking Jerry's mug and setting it on his tray.

He'd never seen a crowd this large at the Salem Queen before. As he moved away from the heavy smoke near the elevator, the full room came into view, and it was packed.

The entire floor was filled with chairs. This was the party room, after all, and it was one of the grandest spaces Haney could ever imagine. Some of the guests had pulled the large, leather chairs into circles. Others, Guerendet among them, gathered around the poker and billiard tables, for gentlemanly games that always ended with someone being cursed or losing a valuable artifact.

Haney heard his name being called from over by the grand picture wall. His heart pounded in his chest when he saw who the voice came from.

Anastasius Fairchild. Sitting next to the wall of pictures, he held the massive chain leash of his pet Mingwa, which roared violently for Haney to come closer. The Collector's table was a crowded one, with everyone from Juskk Borglayo to the Valli sisters trying anxiously to rub elbows with the man whose picture adorned so many places on the grand wall next to him. The pictures were those of the winners of the many Big Hunts, and the Collector had won more than anyone else.

Haney was trembling uncontrollably as he reached the table, the Mingwa sniffed him as he approached, licking at him as if to taste him. The Collector's eyes were dark, almost black, as he made his request.

"A piece of meat for my companion," he muttered, yanking the chain slightly, signaling the Mingwa to growl. It did, and Haney nodded his head as he quickly backed away. The Collector's entire table was laughing at Haney as he scuttled.

The room was filled with monsters, but Anastasius was the one that scared Haney the most. Still, it was a frightening bunch, as in the case of the giant muscular red figure known as Vicade, who stood near the center of the room, enjoying a glass of tea while speaking with Andre Deschaul, a thin dressed all in black with green skin and yellow eyes. Haney had heard that Deschaul came from a long line of sorcerers. Snod had once gurgled to him that they were both serious competitors to Mr. Guerendet, who was yucking it up at the bar with that old geezer, Maxim Rohmer—a frail, bald, elderly gentleman who wore dark sunglasses and kept an oxygen mask in his hand, which he breathed into periodically.

As Haney passed their table, someone from another nearby seat grabbed him, pulling him close.

Rem Tullock.

"Does Anastasius seem to be in good spirits?" Rem asked quietly. His daughter, Amali, sat beside him, engaging no one in conversation but studying the room.

"Everyone at his table sure is having a good time," Haney whispered back, "but

Anastasius Fairchild seems to have something on his mind, I think."

"When is that ever not so," Rem irritably muttered, letting go of Haney's sleeve.

Haney brushed past the rest of the crowd and finally entered the lower-level kitchen. Kibbett the Cook, a seven-foot-tall monolith of a chef, stood next to the stove, slicing carrots into a large boiling pot. He was humming through his thick beard as Haney came in.

"It's about time you showed up. Ice fishing with your boy, again?" Kibbett mused. "That's got to be worth a fever or a nose bleed or something."

"Yeah," Haney said, practically ignoring him,"Listen, the Collector wants some meat for his big cat. Whatcha got in the freezer. Some steer? Maybe a lamb?"

"Nope," Kibbett smiled, walking over to the freezer and opening it. Inside, Haney saw a shivering young man in a business suit crouching on the floor of the freezer and mouthing the word, HELP.

"He came through the rip this morning. And since I've already cooked everything else, looks like the only piece of raw meat we have is little Norman, here," Kibbett chuckled.

Haney didn't know quite what to say, and

Norman squeaked his disapproval.

Out in the party room, the elevator lowered. Its doors opened, and through the smoke, stepped Demira. She ushered in one of the most mysterious figures ever to enter the Salem Queen.

The being stepped through the wisps of smoke. He wore gray jungle fatigues and a black mask that completely covered his face. No eye holes. No slit for the mouth or nose. Nothing but black. His presence immediately silenced the room.

He, Demira, and another creature, frail-looking, with gray flaking skin and a white turban, moved through the room. The room was dead quiet as the impressive gentleman passed Anastasius, the Collector's Mingwa lowering its head as they went by. They walked to the middle of the room, where Demira cleared an area from which to speak.

"Distinguished guests," she announced, "this is your host."

"Hello, everyone," the black-clad creature spoke. "Thank you for coming. I am your host. It is my invitation that has brought you all here. I have devised a contest in which only the world's most fantastic treasure hunters could compete. It is a game to be played in three stages. You will be transported to the first prize's location, and the one to uncover it wins that phase. The second and third stages will work the same way. Once all three prizes are collected, a final winner will be determined. It is my suspicion that, by the end of the last round, there will not be many of you to choose from. You will be expected to deal with each other using any force necessary to attain your goal. I will not interfere. As host, I am but a mediator and director of what will surely be the ultimate contest. Once it is over, I will determine the winner based on achievement, and that hunter's picture will go on the great wall as The Greatest Hunter of This Time. This is my sole purpose as well as my reason for calling you together. This game will determine who among you is the best at what they do. As a favor, I will let you all meet with your trustees to decide if you wish to participate, and in a short time, those wishing to be part of the game will sign the register and enter this once-in-a-lifetime competition. I leave you to your decisions with a promise—the greatest game of all awaits you."

Then, as suddenly as he came in, the host left the room, disappearing through the smoke that had seemed to have suddenly thickened. The room was still in a state of uneasy silence.

THE WILDCARD

Morgan felt something gnawing at his gut as he made his way home. It was guilt, he supposed, but he knew it was something he had to overcome. He was feeling guilty for barking orders at the others. He'd never talked to them like that before. He'd always been a friendly guy-in-charge, never handling his team like a platoon.

But maybe Norbu was right. If the group had a stronger leader, maybe they wouldn't fight as much as they did. Maybe they could become a better team. But a good team needs a strong leader, and if Morgan was going to be that leader, it was time he did something.

Even if it meant ruffling Skinny Joe's feathers. As swelled as that kid's head had gotten lately, he deserved to be put in his place. Morgan decided not to dwell on it.

When he reached his house, he noted that the family car was not in the driveway. He ran up the porch steps, went inside, and discovered no one was home. He assumed his parents and his sister Kelly, had gone somewhere together. Morgan decided to continue his study of the Apa Tuni ceremony while waiting for them to get home.

Flipping on his computer, he instantly saw his e-mail prompt flashing. Someone had sent him a message. Opening the file, he read a return address he'd not received mail from before.

The e-mail was from someone named Preston Talmalker. It was short and to the point.

I know your secret. Meet me at the Fairfield Train Depot at 3:00 P.M.

Morgan checked his watch. It was 2:35. He shut off his computer and hurried out the door.

ENTER:
PRESTON TALMALKER

The three o'clock train was departing as Morgan reached the depot. It roared out of the station, leaving a handful of people milling about the old depot building—the ticketmaster, a janitor, and three people who had put their loved ones on the train.

Not one of them looked like a Preston Talmalker.

As Morgan looked around the station, he noticed that the old Fairfield Express Engine was tucked away on a service track under some trees. It was almost as if the railroad people were trying to hide the historic antique. Morgan was reminded of his friend Elizabeth Martin's encounter with a spirit that haunted the old engine. Her ghost story must have spread to cautious ears, because now the engine, which used to be a tourist attraction, was being hidden away like a dirty secret.

Then, Morgan saw someone lean out from the side of the old engine and motion for him to come.

"Preston Talmalker, I presume," Morgan muttered, trotting down the depot steps, and cautiously making his way over the tracks. He walked over to the engine, and his three o'clock appointment opened the door to the antique passenger car from the inside.

"Please, step in," Preston said.

Morgan felt a shiver of dread just by looking at the kid. A mop of unkempt black hair. Dead, olive-colored skin. And big, thick eyebrows—*too* big and *too* thick for a boy his age. Morgan stepped into the car as Preston strolled about halfway down its aisle. Morgan kept a safe distance between them.

"All right, . . . *Preston* is it?" Morgan asked.

"That is my name," Preston answered dryly, with a touch of contempt.

"So, Preston, what is this secret you know so much about?" Morgan demanded, getting right to the point.

"You can take the form of a Gargoyle at

64

will. Your friend Frank Dunk can become a huge snake. His little brother can transform into a creature some cryptozoologists have classified as a Nandi. I won't bother listing your other five fellow shifters, but all of you know a creature that has been frequently sighted around this area. No one seems to agree as to what it is, but I know it's a Buru. Anyway, all of you have been involved in some significant supernatural happenings around these parts over the last year."

Morgan kept a poker face.

"Sounds like you've got quite an imagination," he said. "Did your parents have any kids that they didn't drop on their heads?"

Preston crossed his arms, nodding at Morgan's remark as if he'd expected it.

"I do not wish to blackmail you," Preston said. "I wish to join you."

"I don't think you—"

"Listen to me," Preston urged, taking a small rock out of his pocket. There were symbols scratched into the top of it. "I'm a student of the supernatural. I've been exposed to many things. I'm very handy with runes. They're Norse symbols that—"

"I know what they are," Morgan interrupted. "Listen Preston, I don't think you've—"

Suddenly Preston disappeared.

Stunned, Morgan realized he'd only blinked and the weird kid was gone, no sign of him anywhere.

"Preston?!" Morgan yelled, and almost cried out when he felt a tap on his shoulder. He spun around to find Preston staring back at him with a grin.

"How did you do that?" Morgan asked.

"You have your secrets, and I have mine," Preston said. "But I'll share if you let me join your team. Please don't tell me it doesn't exist, Morgan. I know it does."

Morgan regained his composure.

"You're a spooky kid, Talmalker. I'm afraid I'll have to get back to you. You caught me on a real bad day."

"When?" Preston asked.

"When I can," said Morgan, opening the door and stepping out of the car.

From the passenger car's dusty window, Preston watched Morgan hurry away. He was confident that he'd hear from Morgan sooner than the boy imagined.

CONFLICTING VIEWPOINTS

When Morgan returned home, his parents and his sister were still not back. He made his way up to his room and found his e-mail prompt flashing once again.

"Give it up, Talmalker," Morgan muttered as he sat down at the monitor. But when he called up the message, he recognized the address as Skinny Joe's.

"Now there's someone I haven't gotten a lot of mail from lately," Morgan said as he began to read.

Morgan, I still think we should give this contest a try. We could gain a lot of information about this circle that we seem to be competing with all the time anyway. Once we're finished with the contest, we pop over to Africa.

What do you say?

Joe

Morgan sighed and typed:

I've already made my decision. It's too dangerous, and we don't even need to be involved. The trip to South America is the important thing here. Sorry.

Morgan

He hit the send button and got up from his chair. He had just stretched out on his bed when the phone rang, making him practically jump out of his skin.

"Hello?" Morgan asked, picking up the receiver.

"You're not even going to consider it? Not even for a second?" Skinny Joe's voice asked from the other end of the line.

"Joe, all you want to do is get there and show off by letting everyone see how many monsters you can kick around. Well, I've got news for you—you've got a bad encounter coming up just like the one Darren had, and that's going to bring you back down to earth—that is, if it doesn't kill you!"

"Morgan, I can count a dozen times I pulled your fat out of the fire! Just because you're our leader doesn't mean you really know the team! I'm ready for this thing!"

"I said no, Joe," Morgan said flatly.

"And that's your final decision?" Joe asked.

"That's my final decision."

"Coward," said Joe and hung up.

Morgan kept the receiver in his hand and used every bit of self control he possessed to keep from throwing it across the room.

THE TROUBLEMAKERS

"So, you're not going?" Darren asked, as he died in Level Five of Werewolf Hunter. GAME OVER flashed across the screen.

"Nope," David said, as he lay on the bed reading one of Darren's many issues of *Kid Cosmos*. "I'll leave this one to you guys."

"I'll tell Rilo that these things are getting too dangerous for you. Besides, I don't think he'd expect you to march in there with us since you don't have any powers," Darren replied.

"You make it sound like a bad thing—not having powers," David remarked, closing the comic book and sitting up. "What I'm scared of is this, if things keep getting tougher like they have been, one of you guys might not come back from a mission. Darren, it could be you!"

Darren glanced at the words GAME

OVER, still flashing.

"So you don't think I'm good enough to stay alive?!" Darren snapped at his brother.

"No, I'm saying it could be any of you—but look what happened with you and that other Werewolf! Geez, Darren, he could have ripped you apart!"

"The lucky bum caught me by surprise! It won't happen again! With him or anyone! You know, maybe it's good that you're not coming after all! I don't need anyone there who doubts my ability!" Darren snarled, getting up in a huff.

"Darren, don't act like a baby! I'm just saying—"

Darren marched out of his bedroom and down the stairs. He had to get some fresh air.

Grabbing his coat, he flung open the front door and walked out into the night. He was surprised to meet Skinny Joe coming up his driveway.

"Hey, what's up?" Skinny Joe asked.

Darren rolled his eyes.

"My brother's a dip. And if I had one wish in the world, it would be to get a rematch with Malcolm Gott!" Darren exclaimed, curling his hands in the air, as if he were choking the life out of an invisible demon.

"Well, I've got a way we can make that wish come true," Skinny Joe's voice became almost a whisper.

He had Darren's attention.

"Frank, are you in there?" Hank called, peeking into his brother's room. The door squeaked as he pushed, the hall light creeping into the dark dwelling as if it were afraid.

"Not now, Hank. I'm brooding," replied a voice from the black void.

Hank flipped on the light switch.

Frank was sitting in his tall, black-cushioned antique chair. The one with snake heads carved into its wooden back. The sudden light made the young genius squeeze his eyelids shut and silently curse his brother's name.

"Hank, bad things will happen to you for doing that," Frank threatened, rubbing the spinning circles from his eyes.

"I-I'm sorry. I was just wondering . . . is something wrong. You've been in here ever since we got back from the manor."

Frank stopped rubbing his eyes and began stroking his chin. His fingers drummed on the arm of the chair as he prepared to share his thoughts with his annoying little brother.

"'I do not like this Norbu character," Frank said.

"Why?" asked Hank. "He's Rilo's buddy!"

"Do *you* trust him?" Frank asked. "Your instincts are unfiltered by logic."

"Well, no. I don't trust him. But he's Rilo's buddy!" repeated Hank, a little giddy that his brother had asked him what he thought.

"Why don't you trust him?" Frank inquired.

"Well, because, uh, *you* don't trust him!" Hank answered, unprepared for his brother's verbal test.

Frank sighed, dropping his forehead into his open hand.

"My word, Hank. You've *got* to start thinking for yourself. I—no, forget it. I give up on you, Hank."

Hank's anxiety level shot up two hundred percent! He'd failed his brother's test!

"But I—"

"Leave me now, Paunchy boy," Frank commanded, as his jackal-shaped phone cackled to life. He picked up the receiver.

"Dunk House. *Oh, hello Kim*! Why yes, I do (ahem) like Jim Carrey movies. He's not just funny, he's crazy funny. Tomorrow night? It's a strong possibility I might be free. I have something to do in the morning, but I may be finished by nightfall . . ."

Hank left his brother's room with his head hung low. Since his brother started seeing their new neighbor, Kim Ling, Frank hadn't had much time for him. And when he did, there was always some kind of test involved. It was almost like his brother wanted Hank to prove his worth or something.

Hank shuffled down the stairs and moped into the kitchen for a Paunchy Boy Pudding Pop and a glass of Grapezilla.

After slurping down half a gallon of the stuff and acquiring a purple ring around his mouth, Hank put his glass in the sink and noticed movement outside the kitchen window.

Skinny Joe and Darren were walking down the sidewalk, passing his house. Hank hurried out the kitchen door and ran to catch up with them. When he did, Skinny Joe quickly filled him in on the plan. Making the decision to formulate his own answer and prove his worth to Frank, Hank chose to join them.

"Okay, let's do it," Skinny Joe told them.

"Do you think we'll be court-martialed for this?" Hank asked, as the three of them stood at the face of the great steel door, in the basement of Fairchild Manor. Behind the barrier lay artifacts so powerful they defied imagination.

"Rilo can't court-martial us," Darren explained. "He doesn't have the military rank to do that. But he could turn us into a bad school lunch."

"Will you two cut it out? Rilo and the others aren't going to do anything to us because we're going to show them who the real warriors of this team are. When we get back from this, they'll want us to lead group missions from then on!" Skinny Joe told them as he and the other two marched to the steel door.

They looked at the formidable barricade, studying its structure and reviewing ways of breaching its security.

"Okay, who set up the new security spells on this thing?" Skinny Joe asked.

"Frank did," Hank replied. "I sat upstairs and ate pizza with Rilo while Frank put up the new barrier."

"Great," Skinny Joe sighed. "Your brother lives for this kind of thing. He thinks about unbreachable fortresses all the time. There's no way we'll be able to crack his code."

"Wait," said Darren. "I was reading an issue of *Kid Cosmos* the other day where he had pretty much the same problem. The evil sorcerer, Lord Neptune, had used magic to take over the Kid's asteroid base by melding with the computer system. Kid Cosmos figured that even with Lord Neptune's new security defenses, there was a back door to any system. He found it, got in, and defeated that sorcerer."

"What was it?" Joe asked.

"Jelly rolls. Lord Neptune's favorite snack," answered Darren.

"Whitefish!" Hank yelled, then slumped when nothing happened. "Well, that's his favorite snack . . . "

"But not his back door. Think, Hank, think. Find an answer," Joe urged.

Suddenly, Hank had the answer. He looked up and sighed.

"Paunchy boy," he said.

There was a thunderous lurch, then the

steel door swung open, revealing a host of glowing artifacts inside. The boys ignored them. The
one they wanted was beside the door. Hank
grabbed it. Once they had the Ceques sliver, they
pushed the steel door shut again for fear of being
exposed to the artifacts for too long.

Skinny Joe frantically dug the invitation
out of his pocket.

"Here's the location," he said, "now give me
the Ceques, Hank. I'll open the rip."

"I can do it," Hank argued, drawing the
Ceques closer to his chest.

"Hank, let one of us do it," Darren told
him. "You'll mess it up, and we'll end up a hundred miles above Earth or something!"

"No, we won't," Hank snapped, "I can do it!"

"Gimme that, Paunchy!" Skinny Joe
snarled, grabbing for the Ceques. Hank lurched
back, squeezing the magical transporter and
powering it up. Joe almost had his hand on it as
the rip opened below them.

Each boy screamed as he fell into the light.
Hank lost his grip on the Ceques sliver, and it
dropped to the floor just outside the rip as all
three boys disappeared.

IN THE MOUTHS
OF WOLVES

Bright light filled their entire field of vision. They felt the incredible but familiar strong wind rushing over them, heard the faint crackle of lightning in the distance. Suddenly, the light seem to pull color from everywhere, pooling it into one spot, then shoving all three boys through it.

The rip ejected them not on the floor, but seven feet above it. They came crashing down on Snod and Jerry's table, splitting antique wood and sending milk and Fresca flying.

"Somebody's throwing kids at us!" Jerry exclaimed, as Skinny Joe, Darren, and Hank tumbled and rolled over each other, desperately trying to get to their feet.

When they finally shot up, all eyes in the room were upon them.

"Heh . . ." Skinny Joe could only chuckle

dumbly as he saw the most horrible faces he'd ever seen staring at him.

Some faces were familiar. Guerendet's. Vicade's. Some, like the man in the beret and aviation goggles (Jussk), or the old man with the oxygen tank on his back (Maxim), were complete strangers to him. The room they were in looked like a supernatural shriner's club. There were things mounted on the walls—skeletal Mingwa jaws, stuffed Yetis, and giant thunderbird bones hanging from the ceiling. There were tables all around, with smoking drinks and bowls of squirming food.

When Hank spotted the Collector toward the back of the room, he innocently waved at him, as a friendly gesture. The sudden movement of the crowd snapped the boys back into the grimness of their situation.

A frantic babbling came over Darren .

"Okay, stay back! All of you! You don't want to mess with us!" he yelled, then tried to transform into his Werewolf form. Nothing happened. He blinked in disbelief, and his heart started racing even faster than before. "Uh, J-Joe, we've got a problem," Darren squeaked. "I can't transform!"

"Now's not the time to be acting silly, Darren!" Joe snarled, then mentally commanded his body to shift. To his horror, he remained human. The blood in his veins practically froze as he saw the crowd moving forward. Something in Skinny Joe's mind snapped, and he, too, started to babble. "Stay away, we mean business! If any of you want some, we're here, ready, and waiting! How about you, Mr. Green face?!" he yelled, pointing a trembling finger at Andre Deschaul. "Or what about you—the guy sucking air?!

Maxim smiled slightly at the boy's idiocy.

Guerendet just shook his head. Vicade sipped his tea, enjoying the show.

The Collector sat quietly at his crowded table, stroking his Mingwa and noting to himself that the children from Fairfield had also received invitations.

Scared for them, Amali started to get up, but her father grabbed her wrist, shaking his head.

Finally, Demira slinked her way to the front of the crowd.

"I am the hostess, here. My name is Demira, owner of the Salem Queen. There are certain powers that will not work here, since once you are inside the Salem Queen, you are on neutral territory. There are no battles allowed here. This is a place of relaxation and amusement.

Now, I take it that since you are here, you received invitations to the Hunt?"

The three boys nodded silently.

"Then, please, stop causing a disturbance, no matter how amusing it is, and simply sign your name to the game register. The Hunt is to begin very shortly, after a fine dinner, of course," Demira said, then turned and walked away.

Darren, Skinny Joe, and Hank looked at the smiling faces of the ghoulish crowd around them, then looked at each other with serious doubts.

"Hey, little guys, glad you could make it," Jerry said, putting his arm around Hank. "Since you fellas are new around here, I'll show you where the sign up area is."

Jerry ushered them through the crowd as conversation resumed. But as they moved among the tables, the boys felt the calculating glances of the other contestants.

"W-What are they all saying?" Darren asked sheepishly.

"Aw, don't worry about it," Jerry told them. "They're just making bets on who's going to kill you first."

The boys, for the first time since they'd landed at the Salem Queen, were silent.

PANIC AT FAIRCHILD MANOR

Rilo and Norbu climbed through the attic window and stalked through the house, on the prowl together again.

"I'd forgotten how much fun it is not to use a door," Rilo said, as they crept down the stairs.

"They've domesticated you, old friend! Didn't you feel invigorated out there? Hunting game just like we used to?"

"It was like we never left," Rilo answered.

"Only, I wish you would've actually let me finish the hunt! I had that deer for sure!" Norbu complained.

"I've lost my taste for wild game, Norbu! I want you to try my new favorite—pizza! I'll call and order one for us now!" he chuckled. But suddenly, Norbu threw an arm against Rilo's chest, his Buru nose in the air. "What is it?" Rilo asked.

"Can't you smell them? My, your senses have dulled. The children, Rilo. I smell the children. They are here!"

"Which ones?" Rilo asked.

"The skinny one. And the young brother with curly hair. And the short paunchy one!" Norbu sniffed.

"*Oh no!*" Rilo panicked, immediately putting things together in his head.

"What is it?" Norbu demanded, as Rilo tore down the hall and into one of the rooms. Norbu followed him inside, down more stairs, and into a well-lit area. It was a large study, and it was empty. Except for the metal sliver that lay on the floor. Rilo walked over and picked it up.

"Those numbskulls. What were they thinking?" Rilo said to himself.

"Rilo, what's going on?" Norbu asked.

"Everything just changed," he said and picked up his phone.

An hour later, Morgan was at the door, and shortly afterward, the rest of the team arrived.

"THEY DID WHAT?!" David yelled, grabbing his head as if it were about to explode from the news.

"Now, calm down, David," Morgan urged,

"don't do anything crazy." He tried to place a calming hand on David's shoulder, but the older Donaldson staggered around in a disbelieving daze.

Michelle struggled to comprehend her missing teammates' level of stupidity.

"Of all the selfish things to do," she muttered as she walked past Frank, who had remained silent upon hearing the news, letting possible outcomes and actions play out in his head.

"If what Rilo has told us of these games is true, they'll never survive the first five minutes. Our only chance is to get in, grab them, and get out. I blame Alister and Donaldson for this."

David stopped his directionless milling.

"Donaldson's to blame? Donaldson?! I don't think so, Eggbert! You've been warping your little brother's mind since the stork dropped him on his head in front of you! As a matter of fact, that little loon is probably the mastermind behind this whole suicidal excursion!" Darren yelled, as Shelly, arms crossed, slowly shook her head behind him.

"Let's not lose our grip on reality here, David. Hank needs help opening a pudding can. It was more than likely Skinny Joe's idea. Morgan really ticked him off earlier today," she said, turning to her team leader as he examined the Ceques sliver.

"I was hoping he'd listen to me. I never expected him to do something crazy like this. I wonder why they left the Ceques behind, though," Morgan asked. Kyle, who had been leaning against the wall, snorted with disgust.

"They were probably leaving it behind just in case any of you chickens wanted to join them. Man, I knew I should have just gone to that contest and not listened to you. Now those three wimps are going to have all the fun! I should have my head examined!" he growled, as Rilo stepped away from the steel artifact door and moved past him.

"Take it easy, Banner," Rilo said, taking a position beside Morgan. "Kids, we have to decide our course of action, here."

"I'll tell you our course of action!" David loudly informed them. "We're going after Darren! My brother's going to have about five seconds to live when this thing starts!"

Michelle squeezed David's arm in an attempt to calm him.

"You're right, David, of course. We go in, save them, then get right back out," Rilo said, slightly turning his head toward Norbu, who had taken himself out of the arguments and sat on the stairs. "Then, we go as planned to save my tribe."

Norbu jumped down from the stairs. The others watched him, ready for him to erupt in a rage over putting the humans' rescue before the Burus'.

"If that is your decision, Rilo, then it is the wisest," Norbu said, surprising everyone in the room. "I will go also, and fight by your side in saving your friends."

Everyone was silent for a moment, until Frank finally spoke up.

"Listen everyone, if we're going to save these three dolts, we need to leave now."

"Frank's right," Morgan agreed. "Is everyone prepared to go now? This is our best chance to get in and out quick!"

"You bet!" David exclaimed. "Let's do it now!"

"Let's go get them and *kill them*," Michelle remarked.

"My, you're caring," Shelly replied, sneering at Michelle, "I say we go and leave *her* there!"

"Let's just go kick some butt," Kyle growled.

Just then, an unfamiliar voice rang out from the stairs.

"Could I offer my help, as well?" Preston Talmalker called, as he descended the stairs. Everyone stood as if frozen in place, attention focused on the intruder.

THE INTRUDER

"Talmalker," Morgan groaned. "What are you doing here?"

"I followed you, in hopes that you'd change your mind," Preston said, stepping cautiously down the remaining stairs. Norbu crouched in attack position, ready to rip the newcomer apart at the slightest sign of danger. "Oh, wow!" continued Preston. "Is this Rilo?"

"No, kid, I am," Rilo said, scurrying over to get a hold on his Buru friend. "Morgan, who is this?"

"I'm a friend. Honest," Preston swore.

"His name's Preston Talmalker," Morgan informed everyone. "He's somehow found out all about us, and he got in touch with me today, urging me to let him join the group."

"And you weren't going to tell us?"

snapped Shelly.

"Yeah, Morgan. This is kind of important news, you know?" Michelle added.

"It simply slipped my mind," Morgan argued, "with the others disappearing, it seemed to be the last thing—"

"Sorry, Talmalker," Frank interrupted. "Our group is an exclusive one."

"Even exclusive groups need new blood, Dunk, or they die off. A little transfusion, if you know what I mean," Preston smirked, stepping down to the floor as Rilo moved Norbu away.

"Morgan, is he dangerous?" Rilo asked, sniffing around Preston. The olive-skinned boy didn't flinch, and Rilo looked uncertainly at Morgan.

"Are you, Preston?" Morgan asked, eyeing Preston's large coat pockets suspiciously.

"Only to your enemies," Preston told him, then spoke to everyone. "Let me explain myself. My father is a cryptozoologist. For the last few years, he's been recovering artifacts just like you have. I've been exposed to some of them. I've even learned to use a few," he said, pulling three round red stones from his pocket. Everyone tensed as he rolled them in his palm, and suddenly, Frank's feet left the floor. He was floating three feet above it.

"Put me down, Talmalker," Frank seethed.

"Just showing everyone what I can do, Dunk," Preston smiled, as he rolled the stones again and lowered Frank to the floor.

"That's great Preston, but we're not taking you," Morgan informed him.

"I think he could be useful!" Shelly said, patting Frank on the back.

Morgan shook his head. "I'm sorry, Preston. Maybe later we can discuss this but—"

"Let him come with us!" Kyle interrupted. "We may be shorthanded without the other guys. We can't form the sphere without them. This guy's toys could save our behinds if we get in a tough scrape!"

"I agree with Kyle," Shelly said. "We admit that we don't know what we're getting into, and we'll probably need all the help we can get!"

"It's nice to see someone using these artifacts to help instead of hurt for once," Michelle said, "and imagine this—he doesn't lock them behind a steel door, never to be seen again! I say we let him go along. If it gets too hairy, we can always send him back through a rip, Morgan."

Morgan scratched his chin, looking to Rilo for some guidance.

"It's your call, Morgan," Rilo said, crouching beside his old Buru friend.

Morgan took a deep breath, and with his hand tightening around the Ceques, looked Preston in the eyes.

"All right. You can go. If things go bad, I'm sending you back."

"Things won't go bad," Preston smiled.

Frank shook his head insistently.

"Morgan, I have to argue strongly against this. This person doesn't—"

"Frank, I've made my decision," Morgan said, turning and focusing the Ceques on the center of the room. The air split, spilling light into the room at a magnificent intensity.

"Let's go get them," Morgan commanded his team.

HUNGRY COMPETITORS

The frail, gray little man in the turban offered the pen to Hank, who took it in his sweaty, shaky grip. All of the other creatures were looking over his shoulder as his trembling hand hovered over the ancient register. His tongue licked over dry lips as he looked around at everyone watching him.

"Sign your name, boy," the thin, wrinkled creature smiled. "Sign and you're in the contest."

"W-What if I change my mind?" Hank asked.

"Once you sign, you're in. There is no 'changing your mind.' Besides, wanting out once you're in would be pure cowardice. Actually, not signing at all would be pure cowardice," the brown-toothed husk of a man warned.

"Don't be a coward, Hank," Skinny Joe whispered to him. "Sign your name. We'll kick monster tail, I promise."

Hank sighed, and, in really big letters, scrawled his name across the line.

The little gray man smiled and called for the next participant.

Skinny Joe took the pen.

Three minutes later, Skinny Joe, Darren, and Hank were all in the contest.

"Hey, hey, hey, fellas," Jerry said, slapping Hank on the back and rubbing Joe's shoulder, "you're in the big leagues now. How's it feel, knowing that very shortly you're going to be fighting tooth and nail with some of the most horrible creatures on Earth, including me and Snod!"

"I feel a little empty," Darren murmured, holding his stomach.

"Hey, no prob, Curly Q! We'll get you some grub! Dinner is served!'"

A dinner bell brought them, along with all of the other participants, into a grand dining hall with a table at least twenty yards long. Everyone filed to a seat. The boys stayed close together. Hank quickly grabbed a seat between the other two, leaving Skinny Joe and Darren to sit beside some of their competitors.

Maxim Rohmer sat beside Skinny Joe. Joe recognized him as the old man he had so brashly insulted upon his entrance, and immediately turned his gaze to the soup being placed in front of him by the waiter. He took a quick spoonful into his mouth as Maxim leaned toward him.

"Uh, the soup is really good," Skinny Joe stammered.

"It's me, son. The guy sucking air, remember?" the old man whispered. "You're dead in the first round."

Skinny Joe took a bite of bread, but found it hard to swallow. Beside him, Hank loudly slurped his soup.

The Collector sat down toward the end of the table. Hank, ever eager to be polite, could not pass up the chance to acknowledge their long-time acquaintance.

"Good luck in the contest, Collector," Hank voiced across the table. "I hope you do good."

The Collector, insulted at the boy's irreverence, swallowed his emotion and nodded an acknowledgement. Hank smiled and slurped more soup.

Darren rolled his eyes and shook his head at his woefully underbrained teammate. Then, he was surprised when a familiar figure took the seat next to him.

"Amali!" Darren exclaimed and instantly felt the heel of her boot drill into the top of his foot.

"Please keep your voice down," she hissed, as she placed a napkin in her lap. "What are you children doing here?"

"We've come to kick monster tail in the name of Fairfield," he said, tearing off a piece of bread and popping it into his mouth.

"You are living your last few hours, you know that, don't you? These men are the most vicious hunters on the planet. They take no prisoners, and they don't set an age limit on whom they destroy," Amali whispered, taking a sip of her soup, trying to be inconspicuous about speaking with the boy.

"You saw us in the Congo. We took pretty good care of ourselves," Darren remarked.

"I saw a bunch of scared children who barely escaped with their lives. There will be no mercy shown to you here. They will—*what is your little friend doing?*" Amali asked.

Darren looked over at Hank and saw he was in a stare-down contest with Andre Deschaul, who sat directly across the table from the younger Dunk.

"Hank," Darren whispered, "what are you doing?"

"He started it," Hank said, staring into the eyes of the green-skinned sorcerer.

The two stayed like that through most of the soup course, until the waiter brought Andre a Chocolate Yoo-hoo, a beverage he had definitely not ordered. For one brief second, his eyes shifted from Hank's to the unwanted beverage in front of him.

"A-ha! You moved! I win! In your face!" Hank yelled across the table, momentarily halting all other conversation.

Andre glared across the table at his taunting rival.

"You just made an enemy, you miserable little paunchy boy," Deschaul remarked, grimacing as he picked up the Yoo-hoo that had cost him the match and handed it to the waiter.

Amali leaned over to Darren.

"Remember what I said before about you being killed instantly? Well, it's going to be quicker than that," she said. Darren gulped, regret settling on him like a shroud.

AT THE GATES
OF INFAMY

Five minutes before Preston Talmalker had presented himself to the others at Fairchild Manor, Skinny Joe, Darren, and Hank prepared to enter the battle of their lives.

Everyone was corralled in a large activity hall, another sub-level room of the Salem Queen. The area was extremely spacious, used mainly for contests of one-upsmanship. Archery targets lined one wall, while a firing range stood ready on the opposite wall. Large circles were drawn on the floor for hand-to-hand matches, and there were long ropes hanging from the ceiling for climbing contests.

This was the room from which all contestants would depart.

Chatter echoed through the large hall until the doors opened and the Game Master strode in. Everyone gawked at him as he made his way through the crowd, and they opened up to let him stand in their midst. When there was absolute silence, he began to explain what was about to happen.

"I will open four rips," the voice behind the black mask said. "Each team will choose which one they wish to enter. Their drop points will be random, but in the general area of the first prize."

"And where is this drop point?" Vicade asked in his gentlemanly manner.

"A swamp region. The prize is located in the heart of a small village there called Banachuk. A word of warning. The locals are very paranoid and they have their defenses. Not long ago, they discovered the artifact you are seeking, and they're very paranoid that someone will come looking for it soon. In short, they're probably expecting you."

"Local yokels? That's it? There's got to be more to this hunt than that. What's the catch?" Guerendet demanded. Jerry patted his boss vigorously on the back, admiring his pushy disposition.

"There is no catch," the Game Master explained. "The first one back here with the prize wins. The rips will appear at the same places periodically, so you may have to wait for them if your timing isn't right."

"So, let us begin," the Collector demanded, stepping forward out of the crowd.

Darren got the sense that the Game Master was smiling underneath his mask.

"Certainly, Anastasius. Since you were triumphant in the last Big Hunt, it will be your privilege to lead this one."

The Game Master nodded to his frail, withered, turbaned counterpart, who in turn ran his spindly hands over the crusty cylindrical artifact that he held before him.

Instantly, four rips appeared, forming a perfect four-cornered square in the center of the room.

The Collector eyed the Game Master for a moment, then walked to the upper right-hand corner and went through.

The Game Master threw up his hands.

"Hunters! The game begins!" he yelled, calling for the other participants to choose their rips and depart. Every team pulled together and chose an exit, hardly any of them deciding to go through the one the Collector had taken.

"Let's take that one," Skinny Joe said, pointing to the one the Collector had chosen.

"Are you crazy?" Darren yelled, "did you see *who* went through there?"

"Yeah, but he doesn't give an ice cream pop about us! Come on!" Skinny Joe said, leading them to the rip. "We'll follow him, he'll take us to the prize, then we'll pull some razzamatazz on him and grab the prize for ourselves!"

"Razzamawhat? I thought the whole point of this was to kick monster tail!" Hank yelled as they filed through.

As the light settled over him, Darren *tried* to remember why he was doing it, but was too scared to recall that bit of information.

THE
GAME BEGINS

Skinny Joe couldn't see the other hunters that had entered the rip before him, but he had some vague sense that Darren and Hank were just behind his floating body as the interdimensional current pulled him through with tremendous force.

Pressure built up inside his head, and suddenly his ears popped as he felt a warm rush of air sweep over him. Then, he wasn't floating anymore. He fell. Hard.

Fearing a broken neck upon landing, it was a relief for him to hit water. He went in hard, sinking slowly in a thick brown soup. He shot up fast, emerging from the drink and gasping for air. He heard two other splashes behind him.

Spinning around, he saw Darren's head emerge. He, too, was choking on the swamp water in which they had landed. Hank came up after him, brown water pouring from his nose. After a spraying, sputtering cough, the younger Dunk noticed a roar that seemed to be growing louder.

"What's that noise?" he asked, as the three boys saw waves slapping through the water toward them.

"THERE'S ANOTHER ONE, HEWITT!" someone screamed from behind them.

The boys turned to see a small, blue and white ski boat coming at them fast. A red bearded man in a straw hat and overalls was positioned at the front, while another man, with a black beard, was driving.

"BOAT!" Darren screamed, just as he noticed what the man had in his hands.

Suddenly, there was a tremendous explosion, and the water erupted in a splash right next to the boys!

"GUN!" Skinny Joe yelled, diving under the water. Hank and Darren followed suit, hearing another shot as they went under.

The boat came to a stop, and Marlett, the man with the red beard, waved his gun over the spot where the boys had disappeared.

"Did you get 'em, Marlett?" a voice cried from the banks of Banachuk Village, only a short fifty yards from the murky swamp position of the boat. The question came from a burly old woman, her head wrapped in a scarf, a cob pipe in her mouth, and an equally threatening shotgun held in her hands.

"Nope, they ducked under. But they can't stay down there forever!" Marlett yelled back, watching the water for bubbles.

"Well, that fellow in the pith helmet made it to shore over there," the old woman said, pointing to a spot of land twenty yards to the boat's right, "and Marlett, I could've sworn I saw something flying around out there!"

Marlett looked up at her.

"What do you mean, Mama—" he began, just as a dark blur swooped out of the sky and rammed into his back. Marlett went over the side as Hewitt got a good look at the thing. It looked like a bat, but it was huge, practically the size of a condor.

"What the—Mama! Tell everybody they're here! Straight from their Secret Gee-netic Labs! Mama, don't let 'em get our evidence—"

From under the boat came a tremendous

force that struck the tiny craft, launching it into the air and flipping it over. Marlett and Hewitt's mama saw what looked to be a giant alligator—possibly the size of an elephant—emerge from the water, teeth showing as it roared. On its back, there sat a red figure, holding the creature's reins and fully in command.

"Storm the village!" Vicade commanded.

From out of the water, nine of Vicade's sunglasses-clad female employees emerged in black scuba gear and armed with harpoon guns.

Seeing them rapidly approach the village, Marlett and Hewitt's mama dropped the cob pipe from her mouth.

"Everybody! Get 'em! Kill 'em!" she screamed, and from behind the tall, muddy walls that surrounded Banachuk Village sprang more bearded men, wielding more shotguns, which they unloaded on the strange force emerging from the dank waters.

"What is this?" Vicade yelled, as the shots spooked his giant amphibious mount, making it jerk backwards and throw him into the water.

While Vicade's troops ducked underwater, Joe, Darren, and Hank came up for air.

"What in the—?" Skinny Joe gasped, just

before Marlett sprang up behind him, wrapping his arms around the boy's neck!

"I GOTCHA! I GOTCHA!" Marlett yelled, as Skinny Joe transformed into the Black-Hound. Darren and Hank tried to pull the swampland man off Joe, while the water exploded all around them with the shots fired from the shore.

Then, Hank heard a deep, croaking sound and turned around to see a cave with teeth opening and approaching them all. Vicade's giant alligator was moving in.

"Uh, Darren," Hank gulped.

"Hank! Help us! This crazy hillbilly won't let go of Joe!" Darren yelled, as he, Joe, and Marlett splashed about amid the barrage of gunfire.

Just as the gaping mouth was almost upon them, another rip opened just above them all, and more warriors spilled into the battle.

SWAMP MADNESS

Hank saw Morgan fall out of the light and transform into a Gargoyle in midair. The smile had barely reached his lips when a Lyken attacked his team leader, engaging him in aerial combat. Then, Hank saw Michelle, who also transformed and who also met a Lyken enemy. The winged warriors were screeching and flapping in the air as Hank saw the most familiar face of all torpedo from the light.

"Frank!" Hank yelled, as he watched his brother plummet from the sky, land on the alligator's nose, and bounce into the water.

The distraction was all Hank needed. Shifting to Nandi form, he launched himself up, striking the alligator right in the chin. As the alligator roared, ready to strike back, two Buru landed on its head and started digging in with their claws. The alligator shrieked in pain.

"Hank! Get everybody to shore!" Rilo yelled from the top of the bucking amphibian as kids continued to land in the water. As Hank moved back toward the struggling Joe, Darren, and Marlett, Kyle and Shelly dropped in front of him, along with some kid he'd never seen before. He felt them all grab on to his fur as he headed for Marlett.

"Look! Some bearded nut's got Skinny!" Kyle coughed, pulling a flailing Preston onboard Hank.

"Kyle, " Shelly argued, "That's not very nice, he—

"Let go of him, Beard-o!" Kyle yelled, as the younger Dunk moved in to help.

"Let go of *me*, you Gee-netic X-periment Gone Awry!" Marlett yelled, as Hank the Nandi yanked him out of the water with his mouth and flung him away from the dog-paddling Joe and the half-transformed Darren.

"Hop on," Hank said, as Joe and Darren grabbed onto his fur.

The gunshots from the shore had thinned, due to the land invasion by Vicade's troops. The combat-ready females were fighting hand to hand with the Banachuk villagers, who seemed to be surprisingly adept at martial arts. Suspiciously, Vicade himself was nowhere to be seen.

Darren heard someone come out of the water behind him and felt a hand grab his shirt.

"David!" he yelled as his brother used Hank's fur to pull himself.

"You're in trouble, brother. Big trouble," David growled, then coughed up swamp muck.

Hank reached shore, just yards away from where the Banachuk villager/Scubafighter war raged. Everyone crawled to shore and transformed.

"Where do you think this thing is?" Preston asked Kyle, whose massive Pendek form made Talmalker instinctively felt safe.

"I don't know. I guess we'll have to go through them all to find out," Kyle growled, cracking his monstrous knuckles.

"You dolts. It's in that tower, of course," a voice spoke from behind them. Everyone knew it was Frank before even turning to look. He was coming out of the swamp, wringing water from his shirttail. He pointed up.

All eyes looked toward the tall, steel water tower standing high above the village, where five villagers guarded its rail, firing shotguns at circling Lykens.

"Hey, Big G! Look what we've got here!" a familiar voice yelled from the rotted stand of trees just beyond the shore. No sooner had the kids turned to look than a large, pus-covered creature leaped from the brush and tackled Kyle the Pendek. The two figures rolled back into the water as other creatures emerged from the trees.

"Guerendet!" Shelly the Phantom Panther snarled, as a collection of Barghests heralded their leader from the dark underbrush, followed by Jerry.

"Leave it to my Lykens to find the right spot!" Guerendet said, as the Barghests growled, clearing a way for him. The kids stayed back, but were ready to attack. Snod suddenly landed at the owl-like creature's feet with a splat. "Snod! Get up, you show-off!"

"We're not looking for any conflict here, Guerendet. We just want to collect our people and leave," Frank told him, shifted to half-snake.

"Too bad it rarely works out that way," Guerendet sighed, just as his feet started to leave the ground. "Hey. HEY! What's this?!"

"Taking out the competition," a French voice from behind them announced. Suddenly, every creature on that part of the shore lifted in the air, and began to float out toward the water. All but Hank, who floated straight up. Under Deschaul's sorcerous power, the cursing supernaturals levitated above the water, just over the spot where Rilo and Norbu were fighting Vicade's giant alligator. Vicade was still nowhere to be seen.

While Hank the Nandi floated above the shore, he saw a familiar green-faced man appear from behind the trees.

"Care to stare me down, now, Paunchy Boy?" Andre Deschaul laughed, completely in control.

THE RUN FOR
THE TOWER

From his spot high in the air, Hank could see Banachuk Village in all its glory. It lay in the center of a massive mud-walled crater, a circle of tiny wooden huts, connected together by a round wooden walkway. In the center of the village stood their pride and joy, an imposing steel water tower. A steel ladder ran from the wooden walkway up to the middle of the huge water tank, where a narrow path was constructed around the tower. On it, the five villagers were still shooting at the Lykens, and Hank saw Rem Tullock and Amali coming over the mud wall on the far side.

Then, Hank heard yelps. Looking to his left, he saw his friends and Guerendet's forces plummet toward the water. Some landed on top of the alligator and Buru, and some went straight into the murky swamp.

Hank looked to his right and saw Morgan the Gargoyle give the Lyken he was battling a faceful of fire, sending it spiraling into the swamp. The team leader then swooped over to where Michelle the Thunderbird battled her Lyken and kicked her combatant hard in the head, sending it down to join its fellow Lyken. Hank saw Morgan point downward, and saw Michelle dive in that direction. Hank watched her dip low, come up behind Andre Deschaul, and ram him from behind.

Hank instantly felt himself fall.

As he plummeted, he saw that Andre had been knocked just under him and wouldn't have time to move. Hank felt a muffled scream massage his back end as he crashed down into the mud.

"HANK!" Michelle yelled. "Are you okay?"

Hank got up. There was nothing left of Deschaul but the tips of his shoes sticking out of the mud.

"What's Skinny Joe doing?" he asked, pointing his huge head toward the mud wall.

Michelle turned and saw Joe jump from the water up to the shore where the last standing Villagers were fighting off the last of Vicade's scuba squad.

"Joe, what are you doing?" Morgan yelled from the air, but even as the words left his mouth, Skinny Joe the Black-Hound threw the last obstructing Banachuk villager into the swamp and bounded over the mud barricade.

"They're going over, you morons!" Guerendet yelled, swimming toward the muddy shore. "I want everyone over that wall and up that tower! That's where they're going—*the tower*!"

"Oh, no, you don't," Rilo growled, still on the back of the giant alligator. "Norbu, grab the reins of this creature!"

Norbu dove into the water, grabbing the leather reins of the alligator, which floated on the surface of the water. He threw them back up to Rilo, who caught them in both claws and immediately yanked back, hard.

"GIDDYUP!" Rilo commanded, swatting the creature with the reins. The alligator shot forward, heading for the muddy shore at tremendous speed.

"SNODDY! BIG G! WATCH OUT!" Jerry yelled from the water just as his two counterparts, along with a bunch of Barghests, reached the shore. The dog warriors yelped, Snod gurgled, and Guerendet's eyes bugged out of his head as the alligator, with Rilo atop, crashed into the shore. Guerendet's forces were knocked around like bowling pins as Morgan went over the bank after Joe.

He found Joe heading straight for the water tower, where under it, Amali and Rem Tullock were dodging shots from above by the village shooters on the tower.

"Joe, watch it!" Morgan yelled, as he swooped low and knocked the charging Black-Hound out of the way of an exploding shotgun blast that struck the dirt just beside him.

"Stay out of this, Morgan! I know what I'm doing!" Joe the Black-Hound growled as they both rolled. Skinny Joe got back on his feet and started again for the tower.

Suddenly, something erupted in midair. A cloud of green smoke that Skinny Joe couldn't stop himself from running through. Once he did, he rolled and crashed, unable to breathe. His head jerked and twisted as he gasped for air.

Out of thin air, it seemed, stepped Maxim Rohmer. He had camouflaged himself using the mysterious gases of which he was master.

"I told you, boy," he said through the plastic breathing apparatus that preserved him. "You're dead in the first round."

Maxim never saw the Gargoyle's claw.

It struck him from the side, knocking his clear plastic gas mask from his face and sending him to the ground beside Skinny Joe. He, too, started convulsing and gasping for air.

"Joe, are you okay?!" Morgan panicked, landing beside his teammate and trying to hold him still. Joe was kicking frantically, afraid he might die at any moment. "Shift to human form, Joe! It might help you!" Morgan ordered.

As Skinny Joe transformed, Morgan saw Amali pull something from her belt. A blowgun of some kind. She aimed it up at the Villagers on the tower and fired. Within seconds, there were no more gunshots, and Rem Tullock started up the tower.

That's when something erupted from the mud below him, and a massive red arm grabbed Rem's ankle.

"Winning this game's not going to be that easy!" Vicade laughed, emerging from the mud.

ANASTASIUS PLAYS HIS HAND

This is true, thought the Collector, as he launched himself into the air. He'd been watching the entire folly from the safety of one of the highest trees, waiting for the right second to strike. Now, with a mighty leap he soared into the heart of the Hunt, proud of his decision not to bring his *entire* army. It would have been too bulky, made everything too uncontrollable.

This is better, he told himself, as his shadow fell over Vicade's red head.

"Who—?" Vicade managed to growl before the Collector landed a boot in one of the pulsing sacks on the side of his head. Vicade lost his grip on Rem's ankle, but on landing, the Collector grabbed it himself and slung Rem off the ladder.

"So, this is how it's going to be, eh, Anastasius?" Rem asked. Amali ran to his side, firing a blow dart at the Collector at the same time. When it hit him in the shoulder, the Collector grinned slightly, then pulled it out and drove it into Vicade's ankle. The red creature, who was still reeling from the Collector's attack, cried out in pain.

"I'll destroy you for that, Anastasius!" Vicade roared, staggering to his feet and pulling the dart from his ankle.

"You will not have the chance," the Collector said, turning again to the ladder. Before Vicade could argue, another shadow fell over him. And this shadow roared louder than he did.

Amali and Rem gasped as the Collector's Mingwa crashed down on top of Vicade, attacking him with every bit of ferociousness it had. Vicade struggled with the creature, fighting savagely just to stay alive.

Morgan watched in horror, lifting the now-human Skinny Joe (who seemed to be breathing semi-normally now) out of the way of the wrestling beasts, both of whom were emitting cries of pain. Morgan also saw Amali and Rem going up the ladder after the Collector and decided that whatever they were going after, they could have it.

"Are we through acting like gentlemen, Anastasius?" Rem yelled up to the Collector, who had just reached the tower's walk.

"This is not a gentleman's business, Rem. I thought we learned that a long time ago," the Collector replied, not once looking at his competitor, but walking around the tower, finding the hatch to the inside.

Rem saw that the Collector had disappeared around the tower. He wondered if he could still take his old friend in a fist fight. It had been so many years. Sixty? Eighty? He figured ninety as he reached the top of the ladder. Amali came up behind him, and the two of them walked around the tower, finding the hatch open. Rem climbed inside, he felt something grab the back of his cloak and pull him up. Anastasius had been waiting for him.

Amali stood back, pulled a flare gun from her belt holster, and aimed it inside the tower.

"Let him go, or I'll blow the whole tower up!" she cried.

"Rem, please teach your daughter how to bluff. It's one of the most necessary tools of our trade," said the Collector, as he stared into the face of one of his oldest friends, knowing there was more to their encounter than met the eye.

"What are you trying to prove, Anastasius?" Rem seethed, hanging in the air above a vat of fresh, drinkable water. Water so clear that you could see the steel box attached to the bottom of the tower.

"That you're too old for this sort of thing," the Collector answered, staring him in the eyes. "Stay out of this one, Rem. I do not wish to kill you."

"That's no way to treat an old friend, Anastasius," Rem said. "What would your brother think of your threat?"

The Collector flinched at the remark and felt the Rem's weight leave his left hand as the old gentleman slipped through his cloak and dropped into the water below.

The Collector dove in after him.

"WHOA!" Rilo screamed, coming over the mud wall still on the back of the bucking giant alligator. "RUNAWAY GATOR!"

Norbu hung onto the back of the thing's tail, and Kyle and Shelly each clung to a side as the enormous creature bounded over the barricade, barely missing the hovering Morgan and Skinny Joe, rampaged past the Vicade/Mingwa battle, and crashed headfirst into the supports of the Banachuk water tower. Wood splintered as the tower buckled, then began to tip over!

"No!" Amali yelled, leaping clear of the toppling structure.

She landed in time to see the tower crack, then spill water over the barricade and into the swamp. Water splashed high, and the murky brown swamp began to seep over the smashed barricade and into the village. Amali ran over to the steel tank. It was beginning to sink.

Climbing on top of the tank, she edged over to the hatch, where swamp water was rushing in, flooding it.

"Father!" Amali yelled. She saw nothing but swirling brown ooze topped with mocha foam, rising to the hatch like a shaken soft drink.

Finally, she saw her father's head emerge from the whirling murk. Setting the attachment on her glove, Amali fired a grabline into the hatch, and her father snagged it as the tank sank lower and lower. Using her enhanced strength, Amali pulled her father out just as the entire tank submerged. They swam over to the muddy bank and watched the tank go down as Rilo and the rest jumped clear of the alligator as it charged off into the swamp. They regrouped just as a late-coming villager rode past the destruction in his boat.

"You may think you got us, but you didn't get us! You didn't get us at all!" the bearded man, identical to all the others, promised with a shaking fist.

"What is that nut talking about?" David asked, and no one could answer, though they all were shaking their heads.

Inside the tank, as the water closed in on the remaining air pocket, a scaled hand emerged from the water, holding the metal box which all the strange armies sought. The Collector's head rose to breathe what little air was left in the tank, and he heard in the distance a speed boat . . .

Swimming out of the hatch, the Collector emerged from the sunken tank. He saw the oncoming speed boat, and he couldn't help but glimpse Rem's surprised face on the bank. As the boat was upon him, the Collector leaped through the air, coming to land in the boat with the cursing villager.

"You! Another evil Gee-netic weapon of the secret conspiracy!"

The Collector snapped the lockbox open, peering at the glowing metallic pieces inside. Then, he looked up at the villager.

"Out," he muttered, his eyes spitting fire.

The Banachuk villager shut his mouth and jumped out of his own boat. The Collector took the helm and directed the tiny craft toward the rip site— and his first victory.

THE WINNER'S CIRCLE

The armies gathered and returned to their respective exit points. Rilo and the kids found themselves going through the same gate as Guerendet and his men, all of whom had just tried to destroy them.

Once through, Rilo and the others reemerged in the grand activity room, where everyone saw the Collector delivering the metal pieces to the Game Master.

They stood in the center of the great room. The Collector stepped forward from the milling crowd and presented the iron box of metal shards to the Game Master.

"The first round goes to you, Anastasius Fairchild," the Game Master thundered, acknowledging his victory over all those listening. As the Game Master opened the box and surveyed the glowing scraps inside, the Collector peered at the Game Master suspiciously.

"These are very interesting items," Anastasius muttered.

"And you can have them, Anastasius," the Game Master interjected, closing the box. "after the game is over."

The Collector watched in silence as the Game Master handed the box to his small, gray servant. Anastasius Fairchild knew a lie when he heard one.

Amali, watching from the other side of the room with her father, leaned over and whispered to him.

"I've never seen the two of you at such odds," Amali said. "Does it have anything to do with what you said? About his brother?"

"Anastasius and I definitely have a colorful past," Rem said, watching his old friend step away from the Game Master. "For one thing, I buried his brother."

"You never told me—" Amali started, and Rem pulled her away from the crowd so no one would hear. He liked to keep his hidden past just that.

"I will tell you this only so you will know why I watch him. For a time, long ago, I lived in the town he and his brother founded. The town called Fairfield. I was with them on one fateful night when something crossed over into our world."

"Something like the Chipekwe?" Amali asked.

"No. Different. Something alien. Something powerful. It brought items, a supernatural map device and a sword, which Anastasius himself used to slay the creature. Langdon and I pulled his unconscious brother to safety after the harrowing battle."

"But Langdon—?"

"Died a few months after that. Murdered in his workshop," Rem said, eyeing the Collector as he left the chamber. "I arranged Langdon's body in his coffin, burying him with some of his most cherished devices as he'd requested, and after the funeral, Anastasius disappeared from the town."

"Do you think he killed his brother?" Amali asked.

"That I cannot answer. Truthfully, the only ones that could, would be Anastasius and his dead brother."

It was difficult for the kids who hadn't been in this room before to stay focused on the Collector's winner's circle. They looked around the room, realizing for the first time just how many creatures were involved in the Big Hunt. To Skinny Joe, Darren, and Hank, however, this was a regrouping of teams that had been energized and hopeful going into the first contest.

They were all slightly jaded now.

As the ceremony ended, the creatures broke off, hoping to find a way to shake off their losses.

Before Darren could even move an inch, David's hand caught him on the shoulder.

"Okay, now we're gonna have it out!" David seethed, not the least bit fearful of his shape-changing brother.

"David! Look, I'm sorry! We weren't thinking! We were just mad that everyone thought we couldn't win this thing!" Darren explained.

"Darren, did you even get close to winning? If we hadn't arrived, would you even have lived to see the end? I don't think so!"

"Hey, relax," Skinny Joe said, as he strolled

up. "This was all my idea. I dragged Darren and Hank into it! If you want to yell at someone, yell at me!"

"Forget it, Joe," David growled. "Unlike you, Darren knows better than to do something this stupid!"

"Okay guys, cut it out," Morgan ordered, as he approached. "We'll settle all of this when we get back home. I'm going to open a rip, and we'll be back to Fairfield in a flash."

"It may not be as easy as that," Rilo told him. He and Norbu had stayed pretty much to themselves, and Morgan was mildly surprised when his friend actually spoke to him. "In hunts prior to this one, you couldn't leave until the entire hunt was over. If you did, you would be tracked and killed within a year."

"You know," David said, "I'm almost willing to take my chances."

"I'm not," Morgan argued. "I'd rather get through this thing. We don't have to participate, we just have to get through it."

"I have information that may change your attitude," a deep, echoing voice spoke behind him.

The kids turned to see the Game Master standing before them. He was bigger up close than any of them could have imagined.

"I am here to offer you a little inside information," he spoke quietly. "Though this is a contest of prestige, the artifacts I'm asking you to collect *do* have power. They would be a powerful tool to aid you in your quest to free your tribe. And, of course, as I told the Collector, once the contest is over, those who have recovered the pieces may keep them."

Rilo and Norbu listened closely as the Game Master continued. Rilo wished he could see the face under the mask. If he could, then he would know without a doubt if their host was lying to them.

"You would be virtually unstoppable in freeing your comrades from their captivity," the Game Master told them.

Rilo's felt a rush of excitement, but was still cautious of the Game Master's intentions.

"How do you know about my tribe? And how do you know we couldn't save them ourselves?"

"Buru, knowledge is the source of power. And I know that the odds you will face in saving them are insurmountable," the Game Master warned, "You will need this artifact's power. Without it, you will not live through your rescue mission." Then he moved away, continuing through the room as if he were socializing at a community benefit.

Rilo breathed deeply as the foreboding figure departed. His mind raced with questions and doubt. Norbu grabbed him, his eyes wide with excitement.

"This is what we need, Rilo! If what he says is true, our brothers will be freed!" Norbu exclaimed.

"*If* what he says is true," Rilo muttered.

Morgan put a hand on the Buru's shoulder.

"Listen, Rilo. Maybe recovering one of the artifacts and gaining the power to save the Buru could make this whole crazy detour worth it! Maybe we should take the chance . . ."

Rilo shook his head.

"I just don't know if the risk—"

"I say we go in and clobber these guys," Kyle growled.

"I'm with Banner," Preston chimed in.

All of the kids echoed the same sentiments. After a moment of hesitation, even David agreed.

"This is going to be the fight of our lives," Rilo practically whispered, the shock to his system subsiding.

"We can do it, old friend," Norbu encouraged. "We will deliver our Buru brothers yet!"

A signal blared over the speakers.

The second contest was about to begin.

Everyone gathered around the Game Master and his withered, turbaned companion as he announced the location of the next site.

"You will be dropped into the Big City, where you must proceed to 1133 Tenth Street. The artifact is located in an old magic building, in the possession of—"

"ME! That's my office!" Guerendet yelled, instinctively slapping Jerry in the back of the head. "You numbskulls! You morons! It was in my office the whole time!"

"Sorry Big G," Jerry cowered. "Snod and I didn't know! When it came in, you were singing show tunes!"

Snod gurgled sheepishly.

"Shut up!" Guerendet commanded, smacking Jerry again as the rips began to open.

"Ready yourselves, Hunters!" the Game Master called. "The second game is beginning!"

ROUND TWO

The Big City.

A ball of light appeared in the dark alley between Java Jive, a crowded downtown coffee shop, and Slices, a gourmet pizza parlor. No one hurrying past the alley noticed the light as it drifted to a stop, four feet above a large rain puddle. The light stabilized, twinkling like a miniature star, and stretched into a long, snaking line, the ends crackling with energy.

Then, it opened with a blinding flash.

Darren splashed into the puddle face first as the others dropped around him. David landed on top of him.

"UGH! I suppose I had that coming," he said sarcastically, spitting out a mouthful of dirty water.

Morgan climbed to his feet, quickly taking a head count. "Is everybody—wait. Oh, no! Where are Rilo and Norbu?"

"Somewhere else, obviously," Frank muttered.

"I don't see Kyle or Preston, either," Michelle noted.

"We have to find them!" Morgan exclaimed.

"There's no time! Let's go! We have to get to Guerendet's office now!" Shelly demanded.

"How? We have no idea where we are!" David grumbled, rolling off Darren.

"We could follow *them*," Hank said sheepishly, directing their attention down the alley toward the street—where Snod and Jerry were busily brushing each other off.

"NYAH!" Jerry cried, catching sight of the children. "It's the brat pack! What lousy luck—and I didn't even try."

Snod pulled Jerry along, hurrying him out of the alley.

"GET 'EM!" Skinny Joe yelled.

The paranormal partners, the oozing man-thing and the nerdy ex-accountant, ran across the crowded sidewalk and out into the street. With the finesse of someone who had done it a million times, Jerry straightened his red tie, adjusted his glasses, and hailed a cab.

The kids emerged from the alley just in time to see the car door slam shut and the taxi edge out into traffic. The two thugs waved cheerfully through the rear window.

"COME BACK AND FIGHT!" Joe cried.

"We need to follow them, you idiot! Not pummel them into submission," Frank said.

"Well, c'mon!" Shelly cried, her voice changing to an animal growl, her eyes narrowing, glowing red.

"Change here? Are you nuts? What about all these people? Won't we attract attention?" Michelle exclaimed.

Morgan spotted several yellow taxis. "Quick! We'll take cabs!" He began checking his pockets. "Who's got money?"

They all looked at each other. No one said a word.

"No one has any money?!" Morgan yelled in disbelief. "I can't believe this! Do you know what this means?"

"We need jobs?" Hank said.

"NO! It means they're getting away!"

"I'm not going to let that happen!" Shelly growled. Her face stretched into that of a great cat's while her body took on the shape of a golden panther. Her eyes glowed red, and her hands and feet grew sharp claws. Shelly had become the Phantom Panther.

In a flash, she bounded through the astonished crowd on the sidewalk, following the cab with graceful leaps. All along the sidewalk could be heard shouts of "Did you see that?" and "What was that?"

"Perfect. Just perfect," Frank muttered angrily, throwing his hand out in front of him, then letting it flop to his side. "Perhaps we should make an announcement. 'Attention citizens: The freakish monster children of Fairfield have arrived!' "

They all looked at each other a moment, then at Morgan.

Morgan barely hesitated.

"Let's go," he said.

Frank just shook his head.

"What are we waiting for?" Joe cried, his body stretching, his ears growing long and canine-like in appearance. His mouth stretched into a snout, and in less than a moment, Skinny Joe the Black-Hound bounded after Shelly the Phantom Panther, easily catching up with her.

Morgan the Gargoyle unfolded huge, bat-like wings, grabbed David Donaldson in his gray talons, and flew straight up, ignoring the older Donaldson's yells of protest.

Darren the Werewolf chose higher ground as his means of pursuit, bounding to a nearby awning, then to a window ledge, following the cab by leaping from high perch to high perch on his strong, wolf-like legs.

Michelle the Thunderbird spread her golden eagle-like wings and flew up out of the crowd to pursue the taxi, soaring through the concrete canyons of the city amidst the cries of astonishment and pointing fingers of its citizens.

Hank concentrated hard, his brows furrowing, his face reddening, as he tried his best to become the fearsome Nandi.

"Come along, Hank. We have to follow the cab," Frank said, pushing through the crowd while keeping an eye on his flying and bounding friends.

"But Frank . . . aren't *we* going to change?" Hank asked, trying to keep up.

Frank watched the crowd's reactions to the sight of monsters. A Werewolf, bathed in red neon, prowled across the top of a movie marquee. A gray, leathery Gargoyle, flapping huge wings, sailed over the street lights. A snarling, shimmering panther bounded down the center line of Main Street. The sight of the creatures created great panic in some and confused alarm in others. Michelle could very well be right, he thought. Just by being there, they were endangering the crowd.

"I sometimes doubt we'll *ever* change," Frank muttered.

"I meant into *monsters*, Frank," Hank said. It was a moment of surprising insight. It caught the elder Dunk by surprise.

"No. I think not."

"But why, Frank?"

"Because sometimes, dear brother, it pays to blend into the crowd," the older Dunk said, becoming just another harried citizen, rushing along the sidewalk.

PARANORMAL SIGHTINGS IN THE BIG CITY

Perhaps if Rilo had looked over the edge of the apartment building's rooftop, he would have seen his team of monstrous children creating a public disturbance while chasing after a taxicab.

At that moment, however, something else commanded his attention: the glowing tip of an electronic whip in Amali Tullock's hands. He could still feel the blood running from the gash in his claw.

"I said don't move, and I mean it, Buru," Amali growled.

Norbu laid his ears back and his mouth curled with a snarl. He didn't like her tone of voice or the manner in which she spoke to them. Lack of respect and physical pain were things he and his kind had been forced to get used to.

"<I'm going to take that whip and show

her how to *really* use it,>" he barked angrily.

"<No. She's a friend of mine. Let me do the talking,>" Rilo barked in return.

Norbu growled, and Rilo took another step forward, a move that had gotten him lashed not a moment before. "Amali! It's me! Rilo! Remember? Makkal Monard? The fight on the riverbanks? We made a great team." He moved toward her again.

A whip crack, zinging the tip of his outstretched ear, was your quick response.

"OWWW! KNOCK IT OFF!" Rilo yelped.

"I mean it, Rilo. I don't want to fight you, but I can't let you go any farther. Dad has to retrieve those fragments this time. It's the only way we can figure out what's really going on here. The Collector is stronger than when we fought him last. Dad is the only one who has a chance against him, and you know it. You'll only get in his way. "

Norbu grabbed Rilo's arm. "<We need those pieces ourselves, Rilo. It could be the very thing we need to free the others. I can take her out,>" Norbu urged.

"What's he saying?" Amali asked, distrustful of the taller, brown Buru.

"He just said how lovely you are—what a fine representative of her species—"

Another whip crack—off the tips of their snouts.

"OWWW!" they both yelled.

"Flattery will get you both in the hospital. You both stay put until I hear from Father and that's final."

"<We don't have time for this,>" Norbu growled, starting for their tall, slender captor.

"You don't listen very well," Amali yelled, cracking the whip at Norbu's legs, intending to entangle them.

As the tip lashed beneath him, Norbu flipped in the air, tucking into a ball, then landed. He grabbed the whip at its center and yanked hard.

Amali was caught off guard. She stumbled and pitched forward—straight into Norbu's flying kick. The whip handle flew from her scaly, yellow hand.

She fell backward and rolled as Norbu lunged. She bounced to her feet in time to deliver a solid punch to Norbu's narrow chin.

The Buru's striped head snapped back, and he felt his legs go out from beneath him.

Rilo hesitated, not quite sure whom he

should stop. They were both friends, and he was reluctant to harm either of them.

Amali scooped up the whip handle and with a crackling flash, lashed the electrified tip around Norbu's pulsing neck, pulling it taut as he struggled.

She maintained her grip, breathing heavily, then said, "That's quite enough from you. Rilo, call off your—"

She felt the whip go slack as the creature lashed to the end of it sailed through the air toward her. She felt two clawed feet slam into her chest, knocking her onto her back on the concrete roof. The air burst from her lungs on impact. She tried to move but couldn't. Her limbs felt as if they were made of lead. Gray spots swam in front of her eyes.

In less than a millisecond, four razor-tipped claws pressed against her scaly throat.

"NO!" Rilo shouted angrily. "Stop, NOW!"

A Buru claw that was not his own wrapped around Norbu's arm.

For a moment, Norbu entertained the thought of pressing into her throat anyway, despite his friend's objection.

"I mean it. We have no quarrel with her. The Buru have no quarrel with her."

Norbu's eyes narrowed. His chest heaved. His breathing was erratic and uncontrolled. He was more beast than Buru at that moment.

Rilo tightened his grip on Norbu's arm.

Norbu smiled. "<Remember the night we fought the Truro? The blue field. The silver-disk moon. The hunt, Rilo. We were magnificent. The two of us, alone, bringing down the most dangerous beast in the valley. How many Buru and Apa Tuni alike had it dragged to its nest? No one dared go after it. No one dared try to stop it. *We* did. We found it. It still had the Apa Tuni' barbs and nets hanging from its hide. Remember?>"

Rilo felt the glow of pride and the overwhelming energy that the brief battle with Amali had unleashed in his friend.

"<I remember it all too well,>" Rilo said, a claw instinctively moving to a large scar on his side, as if to hold closed an ancient wound.

"<The beast had me in its mouth,>" Norbu continued. "<It had merely to bite down. Were it not for you, I'd have dissolved in its belly. Even from my precarious vantage point, what I saw of you amazed me. We had been friends long before. But I saw you clearly, that night, as you tore into the beast and took it down. I realized I had seen

a legend. Remember the spectacle, when you returned to the village, me draped across your back like a sack, dragging the gray wrinkled hide of the Truro behind you.>"

A small trickle of blood seeped from beneath Norbu's claw on Amali's tightly scaled throat.

"<There's not a scrap of hunter left in you, is there my friend,>" Norbu said.

"This isn't a hunt—" Rilo said, in humanspeak, "—and I'm not a killer."

Norbu looked Rilo in the eyes.

"Then just what exactly are you these days, my friend? You're not a human—" Norbu sprang to his feet and began to walk away, toward the edge of the rooftop. "And you're certainly no Buru."

On the street below, Rem Tullock, Amali's father, steadied himself on his silver-tipped cane and continued to push through the crowd. He managed to go mostly unnoticed in the confusion, staying close to the shop fronts. He hoped this lucky streak would last, at least until he got to Guerendet's office.

It seemed a likely prospect. Guerendet

obviously had his hands full.

"WHOA!" gasped a young man wearing headphones, as he bumped into Rem. He had been too busy watching the street to watch where he was going. "SORRY, MAN! CAN YOU BELIEVE THIS? DID YOU SEE THOSE—"

Suddenly, the young man caught a glimpse of what was under the dark, wide-brimmed hat. For a moment, he stared directly into the silver orb gleaming in Rem's right eye socket. Then, he ran off screaming, babbling wildly. He didn't stop until he reached his apartment on Tenth and Willow, forever armed with the knowledge that all monsters aren't on the street. They're on the sidewalk, too.

Rem shook his head, amused at the young man's response. He was glad to know that even at the ripe old age of 230 he still had a slightly sinister aura about him. With a strong but wrinkled hand, he drew his short black cloak closely to his chest and continued to creep past the storefronts, staring with some concern into the street.

The wide, Big City street was currently the scene of an amazing standoff.

The police cars had arrived, their slack-jawed occupants rushing to the aid of their fellow officers—the officers that floated above the city streets, held by ghostly, blue semisolid hands.

Up and down the street, a dozen or more cops flew about, suspended by glowing, ghostly forms. Rem noted that some of the cops were partially *encased* by the creatures that held them. Their upper halves were still human, although monstrously misshapen, but their lower halves dwindled into vaporous, ghostly wisps. Their faces were stretched tight in expressions of sheer terror, their hair fading to ghostly white. The ground was littered with revolvers and shotguns, dropped by the officers who were too horror-struck to use them.

The spectacle amazed Rem. He had not realized the powers some of these young upstarts possessed. It made him think. If he was fully aware of his competitors' abilities, he would gain the upper hand. Maybe not in the Game Master's contest, *but possibly another*. A game that would be played under his own watchful eye. Under his own rules. At that moment, Rem decided to cease his hunt. Instead of letting someone else pull his strings, he would take this opportunity to study his competition. Besides, if he knew Anastasius, the Collector was most assuredly grabbing the prize by now. So upon that thought, the old gentleman stood watching, enjoying the supernatural circus . . .

Mixed among the cops were an assortment of creatures and unnatural figures. Juskk Borglayo, clutching his brown beret tightly to his head, stared out through dusty goggles from astride his friend and steed, Brakk the Nandi, a monstrous beast that resembled a hairy, black rhino with glowing yellow eyes. They edged forward through the shouting, screaming crowd, nearly trampling Baile Edwards and the infamous Valli sisters, all supernatural hunters with little regard for others. A flying spectre sailed past, knocking Juskk off his Nandi. As he fell, he felt the same loathing as the other hunters for the hideous little man in front of the city crowd.

The little man felt hatred radiating from the crowd, but Guerendet didn't care if anyone liked him or not. He had planted his small, fat frame defiantly in front of a wall of other supernatural contestants. Now, he spat his abuses at the crowd.

"Ah, give it up, people! CRAWL ON BACK TO YOUR HOLES! You're never getting past me, and you're NOT going near my stuff! That's right!

MY STUFF! It's in my office, so that means it's MINE! MINE! MINE, YOU MORONS!"

At Guerendet's feet was the torn envelope that he'd been saving for a special occasion. It had contained a set of spectres that he had sealed away personally over three centuries ago, their anger now a vintage that had ripened to perfection. When Guerendet realized that he had been set down with practically everyone else in the contest, he'd thought of the envelope at once. There was no way he was going to let the other contestants into his place. He'd die first. He had stood his ground against the mob, torn the containment seal, and set the spectres free, creating a nearly impenetrable line of defense. Cops, civilians, supernatural hunters—the spectres didn't care what they attacked, as long as they could attack *viciously,* chilling their victims to the bone.

"Yeah! How'd ya like that, Juskk, you Nandi-ridin' pansy! Welcome to my ghost toast! Have a little chilled Spectre, vintage 1697!" Guerendet howled, the flying blue forms whizzing around him, diving into the crowd again and again.

Guerendet noticed a taxicab heading straight toward them into the fray, civilians and hunters alike dodging out of its way. The spectres rushed through the air, preparing to encase the car. Guerendet giggled with glee over what was about to happen to its occupants. That is, until he saw who the occupants were.

"WHAT! Oh, no! Those idiots! I'll kill 'em! BREAK OFF!" he yelled to the spectres around and behind him. "BREAK OFF! LET 'EM THROUGH, YA VULTURES! LEAVE 'EM ALONE!"

Snod and Jerry huddled together and watched through the closed passenger window as the angry face of their employer whizzed by.

"You morons better get there first!" they heard him yell as the taxi and a couple of other cars broke through the ghostly barricade and sped down the street.

"WHAT WAS THAT?" the cabbie yelled.

"STEP ON IT, CABBIE!" Jerry screamed. "We're wanted men!"

"Grady! The name's Grady, not cabbie, pencil-neck, and my number one rule is Grady Norris don't drive for no fugitives!"

Grady jerked the wheel and swerved toward the curb, cutting off a white Honda Civic and inciting a flurry of furious honking.

"GRUUNNK!" Snod bellowed angrily, ejecting a wad of slime from his mouth.

"WHOA!" Hold on a minute, Grady!" Jerry pleaded—with all the earnestness of a game show host. "We're not wanted by the authorities. Nosiree. Not us."

"Yeah right! Just look at you! Hired goons! You *smell* like goons to me."

"GOONS?" Jerry shrieked, his mouth dropping in disbelief. "OW! OH! OUCH! YOU WOUND ME, SIR! We are professionals. My associate and I swipe—um, I mean acquire—supernatural—er, I mean exotic—items for outrageous fees and rewards."

"Goons!" Grady snorted.

Jerry tried a different approach, offering the driver a hundred dollar bill. "Just get us to Tenth and Maple, Grady."

Grady took the goon's money. "Tenth and Maple? You kiddin' me? That joint's full of no-good, air-wastin', goon garbage. And my number one rule is Grady Norris don't drive into goonville, got it?"

"GRONK!" Snod barked.

"What'd he say?" Grady asked, repulsed by

the sight in the rearview mirror.

"He said he thought your number one rule was to not drive fugitives around," Jerry translated.

"Tell your slimy friend he's going to get a fat lip—I guess?—a fat whatever he's talking out of!"

"Drive, Grady. NOW!" Jerry shouted, his eyes glowing red behind his thick glasses.

The cabbie shut up and did just that.

Jerry turned around and stared through the rear window at the intense scene exploding in the street behind them. Glowing lights and crackles of electricity moved throughout the milling crowd. He saw the revolving lights of more police cars close in from the side streets.

Most important of all, he saw a Werewolf, a Phantom Panther, and a Black-Hound get pulled into the fighting crowd by Juskk and the others, while a Gargoyle and a Thunderbird struggled against glowing spectres, rolling in midair.

"At least we lost the runts," Jerry chuckled. "Nothing can stop us now, Snod, old buddy, old pal. Amigo! Compadre! Gimme some goo."

They laughed and low-fived, and when he was sure Snod wasn't looking, a disgusted Jerry wiped his hands on the seat.

TRUE COLORS

"As delightful as this place is, Kyle, I think we should hurry along," the voice urged. The grimy manhole cover moved, then rose a few inches.

Kyle Banner peeked from underneath, scanning the street. His eyes narrowed with frustration, then opened wide with joy when he saw the signs on the traffic light post that read, Tenth and Maple.

"I don't believe it. We're there! Talmalker! We're there!" Kyle whispered.

"That's really great. Now if you'd move your big ol—"

"There are cars around," Kyle interrupted. "We'll have to wait for the light."

After a moment, the manhole slid to one side, and Kyle pulled himself out. Reaching down, he helped the smaller boy out as well. The drivers of the cars stopped at the light didn't seem to notice the two boys as they replaced the cover and darted to the sidewalk. Kyle noticed that farther down the street, people were cautiously congregating, like curious onlookers at an accident. "That's it! Over there! Across the street and on the corner," Preston blurted out.

"How do you know?" Kyle asked. "Gut feeling—and the address above the door," Preston said.

The faded numbers read 1133 Tenth Street.

"Wait. We should find the others first. Morgan might have an idea or—"

Preston rolled his dark-rimmed eyes. "Give me a break. Morgan couldn't lead a dog on a leash. If he did, the mutt would wind up blind, with four broken legs. Why someone as powerful as you follows that guy, I'll never know. We don't need him. C'mon. Let's go."

"No. We should wait for the others."

"Why?" Preston cried. "They'll just mess everything up. Make it more complicated than it needs to be. We can do this. Let's just pop in, grab the fragments, pop out. Simple as that—"

Kyle's eyes shot open wide. He grabbed Preston's shoulder and wheeled him around to face the wall, doing the same himself.

"What is it?" Preston whispered.

"Getting out of the taxi. Across the street," Kyle barked.

Preston darted a glance and immediately recognized the red tie, the glasses, and the pin-striped shirt on the super-wimp frame. Then, he noticed the dripping mountain of ooze closing the cab door.

"Snod and Jerry? No problem. You can take them, can't you? In Pendek form. I'll grab the fragments. It's no problem. Let's go."

Kyle watched as Preston took off across the street, toward the whitewashed, wooden doorway of the dilapidated building. He could barely make out a faded mural/billboard on the wall beside the main doorway. It showed a fifties-style magician in tux and tails, a collage of magical delights ranging from rabbits to rainbows streaming from his upturned hat. The building apparently had once been Merely Magic®—the magician kit factory. How fitting.

Preston reached the doorway, peeked in at the empty stairs, and signaled for Kyle to follow him.

Kyle rubbed his face hard. His brain sent warning signal after warning signal. Still, Kyle Banner was never one to let his brain get in his way. "All right—But I'm probably going to regret this."

Kyle darted across the street, running up to Preston just as a loud commotion erupted from a fourteenth-floor window.

They looked up in time to see a large, black object crash through the window, shattering the glass. They leaped into the doorway, away from the hurtling object, just as it crashed to the pavement with a bone-cracking THUD!

Kyle knew what it was the moment he saw it.

The smoking, charred remains looked like those of a giant tiger. The hair had been burned black on its muscular body. Its mouth was open, the jaws set like those of a great white shark's with many rows of teeth, capable of swallowing a boy whole, or grinding him into small pieces.

"What is that?" Preston asked.

"It's a Mingwa," Kyle said, looking up fourteen stories to the hole in the window it had made. "This is not a good idea."

"C'mon." Preston darted up the stairs.

Kyle followed closely behind, charging up the stairs after Preston. His footsteps grew louder and heavier as he began to shift. His head widened, his face shrinking between two puffs of leathery skin. His hands stretched and grew claws, and long hair sprouted everywhere, covering him completely. Kyle Banner was now Kyle the Pendek.

It wasn't hard to find Guerendet's office. They only had to look for the door in the hallway that was now a smoking hole—where the Mingwa had forced its way in.

Preston charged over to the former door and boldly stepped inside. Kyle followed, amazed at the kid's bravery—or stupidity.

The office looked as if it had been hit by a bomb. The artifacts, trinkets, rare photos, and clippings that had once decorated the stained walls and chipped furniture lay scattered and shattered on the wooden floor. A ratty, stuffed animal resembling a monkey, only it was six feet tall with no tail, had fallen onto a glass case filled with crystal skulls of varying sizes. Behind the large desk lay the shattered remains of a framed photo of a younger, prouder, more human-looking Guerendet presiding over a top-secret excavation site in Pakistan.

"THE BOSS'S FAVORITE PICTURE! YOU WILL ALL PAY!" Jerry screeched.

He was crouched on all fours behind the desk, while Snod eased his way toward the large, two-door cabinet pressed against the wall near the shattered window.

Jerry and Snod didn't grab Kyle's attention. The other two gentlemen did.

A monstrous man stood near a lamp made of bone. He was nearly twelve feet tall, wearing a black suit of impeccable quality. His blood-red skin stretched over perfectly formed muscle. Two large puffy sacks swept from his forehead to the back of his neck. His eyes were small and flickered with yellow fire. His teeth—small, short, and razor sharp—locked together in a dazzling smile.

"Now that I've taught your kitty to play fetch, let's see if I can teach you how to fry," Vicade growled, his throat swelling, glowing beneath the skin. He was preparing another cloud of fire for his adversary—the only contestant to beat him to the office.

The Collector didn't respond to Vicade's taunting. He didn't come up with a witty one-line retort. He didn't smile or goad or even *try* to look like he held the upper hand. He didn't appear to be even slightly upset at the loss of his Mingwa. He apparently didn't find Vicade very much of a threat. As for Snod and Jerry, the Collector didn't even acknowledge their presence in the room. If there was any flutter of emotion inside his dark, sinister form, he kept it well hidden. His eyes were hard yellow slits that coolly appraised his opponent. His posture exuded extreme confidence, green scaled hands clasped firmly behind his back, just over his wide belt. His black jumpsuit had a tear on the left sleeve—a surprise present from Vicade. A surprise that would be repaid in kind. The Collector didn't even look at the prized metal fragments lying in a wad of packing paper on the desk.

The Collector didn't say a word.

He waited, seemingly immobile.

Like a snake.

Snod reached the cabinet, pulled it open, and tore a short staff from inside. "BRAAACK!" Snod gurgled, aiming the staff back and forth between Vicade and the Collector.

"FRY THEM BOTH, SNODINATOR!" Jerry screamed from behind the desk, poised near a valve control on a large pipe that ran from floor to ceiling.

Both the Collector and Vicade saw Snod before he attacked, but Vicade moved first, lunging toward the slimy man, belching fire.

Snod's retaliation, a ball of flame fired from his staff, met Vicade's and exploded with a tremendous blast, engulfing the red-skinned giant completely. Fire now crawled like a living entity along the ceiling and floor as Vicade staggered, momentarily stunned.

Snod, his sticky skin encrusted with black smoke residue and ash, stumbled backward, gasping for breath.

Vicade had time to turn back to face the Collector before he heard something whiz through the air and felt his throat close. His eyes bulged in their sockets. Something had wrapped itself around his throat. Something like a snake. No. Not a snake. A cord. A dense, black cord had wrapped around his thick neck a dozen times or more, and it grew tighter by the moment. He glanced down and saw two black metal spheres dangling from the ends of the cord. The Collector's bolo.

"Nicely played," he wheezed, before falling

face first to the floor with a tremendous thud.

The fire spread rapidly through the office. Kyle and Preston realized they didn't have a moment to lose.

"KYLE! STOP THE COLLECTOR!" Preston yelled, running for the metal fragments before the flames reached the desk.

Kyle the Pendek did just that. In two leaping strides, he was upon the scaly hunter, his massive claws grabbing for the snakeman's neck.

But in a sudden blur of motion, the Collector's right hand whipped out and seized the Pendek's throat instead. His powerful, vicelike grip nearly snapped the hairy creature's spine as he raised the Pendek from the floor. The bony plates that covered the Collector's scaly skin grew more rigid, drawing closer together, forming a natural armor, impervious to even the desperate Pendek's kicks and punches.

The sight gave Preston reason to pause. The man was easily half the size of the Pendek, yet was holding him out at arm's length, like a doll.

Preston pulled his gaze away and concentrated on the task at hand. He reached the desk and saw the precious metal fragments, glinting in the light from the flames all around them. He touched them quickly and cautiously, to test their temperature. Nothing. They weren't conducting heat. Quickly, he reached for them—but a frail human hand grabbed his wrist.

"Now are those really yours?" Jerry screeched, the flames on the wall behind him nearly as bright as the red glow in his eyes.

"They are now, four-eyes!" Preston yelled, knocking Jerry's glasses off.

"MY GLASSES!" Jerry cried, releasing the boy's wrists.

Preston grabbed the fragments and ran to the door. Snod, now staggering about, grabbed for him but was still too groggy and blinded to connect.

"Those are mine, boy," the Collector snarled, moving toward Preston with the Pendek in tow.

With the Collector's claw still locked around his throat, Kyle felt the room darkening. His lungs strained but could not draw a breath. He could feel himself reverting—changing back to human form.

"Preston—help me," he mouthed, barely producing a squeak.

Preston paused in the doorway, fragments in hand. He looked back at his ex-teammate and smiled. "Sorry, pal. Can't help you. I got what *I* wanted. Time to go solo. Oh, and just between you and me—your little team is history."

"No," Kyle mouthed, on the verge of unconsciousness.

Preston vanished through the doorway in a billow of smoke.

The Collector roared with anger and marched after him, flinging the half-Pendek across the room, sending him sailing into the stumbling Snod.

Who, in the smoke, pain, and confusion, stumbled right out the hole where the window had once been.

"SNOD!" Jerry screamed.

TALMALKER MUST BE FOUND

'This way, Frank! We can see them from over here!" Hank yelled, pulling his brother along the sidewalk. Frank had asked another taxi driver where 1133 Tenth street was, how long it would take to get there, and what kind of neighborhood it was. He didn't like any of the answers.

Now, they pushed along the edge of the crowd that watched the police struggle both mentally and physically against the bizarre contestants. Most of the police officers were fully grounded in reality. They had no time to ponder the existence of the supernatural, and therefore could make no sense of what they were fighting. When traditional tactics, such as reason and bullets failed to work, some chose to shut the bizarre nature of these perpetrators out, hoping to find a reasonable explanation later. Others simply went mad.

The crowds along the sidewalks had thinned considerably with the arrival of more policemen—and a SWAT unit.

The SWAT members, after a confident exit from their large black van, proved nearly as ineffective as the cops. Of course, their placement was more orderly, their approach more controlled. But in the end, the color of their uniforms and the weight of the weapons they dropped were the only difference.

And Guerendet still held them off.

All of them. Every cop, contestant, or creature that tried to get past him or get *to* him found themselves tangled in web of spectral light under his command.

Even Morgan Taylor the Gargoyle.

Morgan and David had tried to go after the taxi but found themselves under attack. The Gargoyle accidentally dropped David into the crowd when he became tangled in a whirling, ghostly web—a web with a shrieking human head.

"DARREN!" Morgan cried, struggling with all his strength to break free, rolling in the air. "GET TO DAVID!"

Darren the Werewolf, currently fending off

a swarm of Barghests, savage bipedal dogmen, heard the Gargoyle's cry and swiftly dove into the thick of the crowd to try and find his brother. He thought he saw David's hand shoot up from behind Juskk's Nandi, but he wasn't certain.

Skinny Joe the Black-Hound and Shelly the Phantom Panther had attempted to bound past the crowd in pursuit of the cab, but found themselves ensnared just as Morgan had been, though on the ground. They rolled and snapped at their ghostly captors, fighting the brain-numbing terror the incorporeal creatures repeatedly tried to inject into their minds. They had the advantage of supernatural bodies and felt bad for the human cops as they faced similar struggles— turning white-haired and going mad as a result.

"MORGAN!" Hank yelled from the sidewalk.

The Gargoyle rolled in the air, and even through the bluish haze flooding his eyes, saw the Dunk brothers, clear of the struggle. "GO!" he yelled. "FIND THE FRAGMENTS!"

"What about you and the others!" Hank yelled, his voice cracking at the thought of leaving his friends in their struggle.

"GO!" Morgan growled. "We can handle

this! HURRY!"

"Come, Hank," Frank said, realizing that Morgan was right. For the moment, the fragments had to come first.

As Frank and Hank sneaked past the Guerendet-made barricade, they saw a Werewolf with an angry young man in tow spring from a Nandi's back.

"Darren, if I live through this, I'm going to kill you!" the boy yelled.

Frank and Hank ran most of the way down Maple Street, heading for the corner where they would surely find number 1133. They were quite sure that Snod and Jerry were there by now. They only hoped that through some miracle, it wouldn't be too late.

Then, Hank saw a faded mural on the side of the building.

"Look, Frank. Merely Magic® Magic Kits! I had one of those!" Hank yelled excitedly. He slowed down, clutching his plump side in pain. His shorts had ridden up and his well-worn gray T-shirt had soaked through with sweat.

"Yes," Frank said, breathing as hard as his brother. "As I recall, you tormented me with that accursed raising cane trick—day and night."

"But I thought you liked that trick!" Hank cried.

"The twentieth demonstration proved annoying—the hundredth, infuriating. Unlike your glob of gray matter, most brains develop a sense of useless repetition."

"You're just mad because you never figured it out," Hank said.

Frank said nothing.

"You're dwelling. Aren't you?"

"Need you ask?"

"FRANK! LOOK! IT'S KYLE!"

It was indeed Kyle. He staggered around from the side of the great, brick building and nearly collapsed. His clothes were blackened, wringing wet, and covered with ash stains. Frank and Hank ran over to help, grabbing him from either side before he fell.

"Kyle! Are you okay? What happened?" Hank asked.

Kyle coughed then grumbled, "Preston happened. He's a traitor. Took the fragments and ditched me. He was going to ditch us all along. Was in it for himself. A regular Benedict Arnold and I fell for it."

"I feared as much," Frank said.

He looked down Tenth Street and saw a charred, black Mingwa lying on its massive back atop a layer of shattered glass. Farther out, a splattered pile of greenish yellow ooze lay atop a pile of black clothing. A nerdy-looking man with glasses and a red tie had fallen on his knees beside the glop and was scooping up handfuls and sobbing.

Then, Frank noticed the charred hole in the wall, fourteen stories up.

"What happened up there, Kyle?" Frank asked again.

Kyle summarized the events: the Collector and Vicade's fight. Snod's fall. How a frantic Jerry had turned a large valve on a huge pipe on the rear wall behind the desk and drowned the entire office, putting out the fire in less than a minute.

Kyle moaned. "The water came out of those sprinklers so hard it hurt. Anyway, it woke me up. In a way—that spastic little loser saved my life."

"Did you see which way Preston went? Did the Collector go after him?" Frank asked, as Hank tried cleaning Kyle's face with a rag he pulled from his back pocket.

"No. I came to, stumbled down here, then you guys found me."

Frank steadied himself, eyeing Jerry, who was scooping up as many globs of Snod as he could find and patting them together, sobbing all the while.

"Frank? Where are you going? What are you going to do?" Hank asked.

"Something I probably shouldn't."

Frank approached Jerry cautiously, as if the slender geek were a wounded lion. "Jerry. I'm terribly sorry about your—loss," Frank said, as somberly as he could.

Jerry looked into the grim, serious eyes of the apologetic young genius who stared under the bangs of his bowl-style haircut.

"He didn't have to do this," Jerry sobbed. "Snoddy and I have been through it all, you know. I have no one else. He was my only—my only friend."

"I know. I'm sorry. Jerry, did you see Preston Talmalker—the boy who took the fragments? Did you see where he went? Did the Collector go after him?"

Jerry didn't say a word, but pointed

toward the warehouse across the street. The door at the top of the concrete steps was hanging open. "It's the old magic kit warehouse. Mr. G uses it for storage mostly, the nonpowered junk—tikis, gemstones, statues, you name it, stuff he got when he was just into straight acquisitions."

"Thank you, Jerry," Frank said, lowering his head gratefully, then running back to Kyle and Hank.

"Well?" Hank asked.

"Preston is in that warehouse," Frank reported. "My guess is the Collector is in there as well."

"I meant about Mr. Snod," Hank asked sadly.

"Oh. Well, as you can see, he's a mess. Let's go. We're running out of time," Frank said, starting toward the warehouse steps. "If Preston is still alive, the Collector will take care of that, as well as getting the fragments."

Hank looked sadly at poor Jerry, who was begging Snod to pull himself together. "Poor Mr. Snod."

Kyle looked confused, clutching his head in pain. "Wait. We're going alone? Didn't I just leave this party? Where's everybody else?"

"Busy." Frank responded.

"Typical."

Darren felt a cold wind whip through him, rippling his fur, as he struggled against the shimmering entity that had entangled him. He saw the tips of the hair on his claws turning white and realized he was losing the struggle. Then a scaly green blur knocked him aside and the bluish swirl of malevolent mist wrapped itself around his new attacker.

"RILO!" Darren the Werewolf growled. "Am I glad to see you!"

Rilo gnashed his teeth and snarled wildly, clawing the spectre with an uncontrolled fury. His eyes glowed as red as fire, and his ears lay flat against his head. He closed his eyes and concentrated, fighting the creature through force of will, pushing its chilling attacks from his mind. The spectre whirled and shrieked, fleeing from Rilo to find easier prey.

"Darren! Where are the others? Did you find Guerendet's office?"

"Frank and Hank are there now, or they should be unless something happened."

Pushing himself off the roof of a police car,

Norbu leaped through the air, sailing into the Gargoyle who was struggling with a wispy blue vapor. Morgan fell as Norbu took his place, attacking the spectre with the same fury that Rilo had shown.

Rilo bounced through the crowd, shoving past Juskk and the Valli sisters. He crouched next to Morgan, helping him to his feet, despite the jostling of others.

"Come on," Rilo said, shouting over the noise of the crowd. "Help me clear the others. We have to find Frank and Hank. Rem and Amali are sure the Collector wants those pieces for something other than the contest. He wants those pieces—badly."

Frank and Kyle pulled the large, sliding metal door to the side and peered into the warehouse. Dust hung like a curtain on the air, and beyond that curtain was darkness.

Hank joined them, and they all stood for a moment looking into the warehouse, their eyes adjusting to the gloom. They saw thousands and thousands of shelves stacked with broken statues, smashed antique furniture, chipped gemstones, and dented metal urns, all covered with shrouds of clear plastic. The useless results of a thousand expeditions. Beyond them were crates and crates of dusty, damaged magic kits.

"After you, smiley," Kyle said.

Frank frowned and took a cautious step inside. "Preston?" he yelled.

The other two followed him in, and they pushed the door closed behind them. Cautiously, they began walking among the towering shelves, scouring the darkness for any sign of the treacherous boy.

Kyle huffed, his patience growing thin. "Let's leave him. Let's let him have it. That wimp will never make it back with the fragments, anyway. Somebody will just take them away from him."

"That's the problem. Until we know what we're dealing with here, it's better if we keep the fragments in our own hands. HANK! Put that down," Frank demanded.

Hank looked at his brother, an old Merely Magic Wand® clasped in his hand.

"Sorry," he said.

They continued to walk along the narrow corridors, scanning each large crate, kicking at every skid.

"Preston!" Frank shouted. "We need to talk. I have a feeling you really don't want what you're holding. You'll never make it back to the rip alive. You're chances are much better with us. People will kill you for it, Preston. People like—"

"The C-Collector," Hank stammered.

"Yes, Hank. Very good," Frank whispered. "People like the Collector," he agreed.

Then, Frank noticed that Kyle and Hank were backing away. He turned his head sharply, and realized Hank's comment had a different meaning.

The tall, shadowy figure—standing only a few feet away—was unmistakable. They could see the glint of his narrow yellow eyes.

"Children," the cold voice rumbled. "I've grown tired of noisy, troublesome children. Tired of their whiny voices, their fidgety forms, their sticky fingers, taking things that aren't theirs— so very tired indeed."

As the Collector drew closer, they could see the rows of bony spikes jutting from his forehead, growing longer and sharper. His teeth glistened as his narrow lips opened with a growling hiss. They could hear the ends of his gloves tearing as razor-tipped claws grew longer.

"We are about to die," Frank gulped.

Kyle agreed, though he was too terrified to say anything. The thought of those horrid claws closing around his neck sent shivers of dread through him.

Then the sound of sliding metal echoed through the building.

"FRANK! HANK! KYLE!" Morgan yelled. "ARE YOU IN HERE?"

The three boys seized the moment and ran, their pulses racing, flying along the rows of shelves until they reached the door, now open as Morgan, Darren, David, Skinny Joe, Michelle, and Shelly rushed in.

"GUYS!" Hank cried.

"THE COLLECTOR IS RIGHT BEHIND US!" Frank shouted.

All eight of them shifted into their monstrous forms, preparing for a fight.

A figure did indeed spring from around the tall scaffolding of shelves, but it wasn't the Collector.

"You pathetic idiots. You've no idea the power these fragments contain," the figure cackled, stepping closer.

It was a Preston, clutching a handful of

metal fragments, eerie green light spilling between his fingers. He began to run straight toward them.

"Outta my way, idiots," Preston laughed. "And be sure to keep the Collector busy for me— if you can."

"STOP HIM!" Morgan the Gargoyle cried, hovering in the air.

The eight monstrous forms prepared to stop the charging boy, but an explosive ball of green light mushroomed from the fragments in the boy's hands, knocking them away to land flat on their backs.

Preston shot past them toward the door, laughing as he ran.

The greenish glow surrounded the others, causing them to revert to human form. They looked around in panic, knowing they were open to an attack.

But the Collector had disappeared.

A SHAKY SITUATION

Still sobbing, Jerry scooped up the remaining globs of Snod, placed them on the ash-stained, V-neck black T-shirt, and patted them down into the rest. On the uppermost glob, he carved out two eye holes and a line for a mouth, as if sculpting runny putty.

"Please, Snoddy. C'mon. Don't leave me here all alone."

The glob didn't move. It didn't even wiggle.

"Snod," Jerry urged, pushing back a long strand of blond, sweat-soaked hair. His eyes glowed with a faint red light.

The glob stared up lifelessly with the crude smiley face Jerry had carved into it.

"Snod!" he said again, more forcefully, his eyes throbbing with red light. He sniffed loudly and wiped a tear from his cheek.

"SNOOODDD!" he yelled, gritting his teeth to the point of cracking. He shot to his feet as if yanked by invisible strings. He turned and faced the warehouse angrily. They were in there. All of them. All of those responsible for the Snodinator's sorry demise.

Jerry's face twisted in rage, flushing as red as his tie. The veins on his forehead throbbed. His tightly balled fists began to shake, and he summoned every ounce of will he could muster. He always had a knack for causing bad luck—for causing bad things to happen, even though he sometimes caught the worst of it.

Well, this one was going to be a doozy.

Preston darted through the warehouse door and fled up the sidewalk as fast as he could go, paying no attention to the trembling, scrawny man overcome by grief and anger who stood in the middle of the street.

Morgan, Frank, and the others emerged from the warehouse—as the first tremor nearly knocked them off their feet.

"WHOA!" Skinny Joe cried, grabbing hold of Darren's shoulder to keep from falling over. "What was that?"

"I don't—" Morgan began, but a loud rumble drowned him out.

The ground shook violently, growing worse by the second. All around them, windows shattered, raining glass down on the street. A street lamp cracked and fell over, the colored lights shattering on impact. The manhole cover Kyle had so recently crawled out of blew straight up on a geyser of steam.

"LOOK OUT!" Michelle cried, shoving Shelly to the side as a large chunk of concrete fell from the roof of the warehouse, cracking the pavement.

Frank and Hank watched rows of parked cars slide as the concrete cracked, shifted, and rose beneath them. "FRANK!" Morgan yelled. "What do you think's causing this?"

Jerry's head shook wildly on his shoulders, his teeth bared between stretched lips. His wire-frame glasses slid down his face and hung off his nose. He screamed loud enough to wake the dead.

Rilo, Norbu, Guerendet, and the remaining contestants at the spectre blockade all stopped a moment, feeling the ground rumble beneath them. Even the spectral entities themselves paused, sensing impending disaster.

Guerendet turned his head nearly 180 degrees and looked down the street behind him.

He couldn't believe what he was seeing with his owl-sharp vision. The pavement actually rippled, like a wave, flipping and sliding cars around like toys.

And the wave was coming straight toward them.

"Jerry," he muttered.

"The kids!" Rilo cried. He and Norbu leaped from the crowd, bounced off the Nandi's back and over Guerendet's head, taking off toward the source of the ripple.

"JERRY! SNAP OUT OF IT!" Morgan cried, afraid to touch the trembling man.

All around them, bricks and glass shards fell from the shaking buildings. The pile of yellowish glop and black clothes that used to be Snod rolled against Jerry's legs.

"HIT HIM!" Kyle insisted.

"YOU HIT HIM!" Darren shot back.

"WELL, SOMEBODY DO SOMETHING!" Shelly yelled.

"Oh, no. LOOK!" Michelle screamed.

A large metro bus careened down Tenth Street, skidding as the pavement beneath it buckled. The driver desperately spun the wheel, but it was no use. One of the parked cars had slid right into its path. The street in front of the two vehicles split, creating a deep, smoking concrete canyon. The bus's brakes locked, and the smoking tires tore against the concrete as the bus smashed into the car, continuing its forward slide. Screams rose from the terrified passengers as the rear wheels of the bus left the ground.

The bus was about to flip and slide into the fissure.

"LET'S GO!" Morgan cried, a signal to transform.

There was a tense moment of silence and dumbstruck realization. They all looked at each other, their hearts sinking, fear racing down their spines.

They were still *very* human.

"Uh oh," Hank said.

THE POWERS THAT WERE

The rear of the bus fell back to the pavement with a spray of sparks. It lurched to one side, and both car and bus dropped into the jagged canyon in the middle of Tenth Street. The rear wall of the fissure crumbled somewhat as they plunged in. A cloud of smoke and debris rose as the vehicles hit the bottom. The roof of the bus was barely visible from above.

The ground continued to shake, collapsing the sides of the fissure even more, the vibrations sucking more cars toward the wide crack.

"NO!" Michelle cried.

"LOOK! IT'S PRESTON!" Kyle growled.

Preston had indeed stopped about a street away, looking back and laughing at the now-powerless heroes. "Bye-bye!" he yelled, running down the street. Next stop: a hopefully open Ceques gate and victory.

"LET'S GET HIM!" Skinny Joe yelled. Darren and Kyle had already started after him.

"NO!" Michelle demanded, stopping them cold. "Those people need help!"

"But—but we don't have powers," Skinny Joe said.

"So what," Michelle shot back.

In a flash, she had run halfway to the smoking concrete canyon. Morgan ran right after her, as did Frank and the others. Shelly was the last to go. She watched Preston for a moment more, then joined her friends.

The bus landed on its wheels, twelve feet down, and there was only three feet or so of space between on bus and the fissure walls on either side. Michelle jumped on the roof of the bus, then dropped down the side to the unstable canyon floor. Twisted metal rods cut her legs and gouged her side. A watermain burst, spraying her with the force of a firehose. Still, she managed to get to the bus door, helping the stunned driver pry it open. One by one, she helped the frantic passengers through the door, guiding them up a pile of debris to Frank, Hank, and Kyle's outstretched hands.

Morgan did the same at the back end of

the bus, helping with the emergency door, then guiding eager hands toward Shelly, Skinny Joe, and Darren.

The ground beneath the bus shook and dropped slightly, sending the bus rocking into one wall and debris raining onto its roof.

"Look out!" Darren yelled. "The walls are gonna cave in!"

"Almost there!" Michelle choked, nearly blinded and strangled from the sprays of debris and water.

Kyle pulled up the last passenger as Frank grabbed Michelle's hands and pulled her free.

Shelly grabbed a younger girl's hands and pulled her up from the debris pile as the side wall collapsed with a crash—then the front wall— then the other side wall.

They had barely managed to stumble out of the way before all the walls caved in, burying the bus up to the roof, smashing the windows and crushing the sides.

Shelly, still clutching the young girl, looked at Michelle with fear-filled eyes, nearly crying. Had they—Was anyone—?

"It's okay! That was everyone! We did it!" Michelle cried.

"We did it," Morgan said, sighing with relief, putting a hand on Frank's shoulder.

"We really did it," Skinny Joe replied, incredulously.

The shaken younger girl turned to Shelly and said, "Thank you."

Shelly hugged the girl and began to cry.

FINDING A RAT
IN THE SEWER

Preston Talmalker clutched his prize to his chest as he ran. The fragments were still glowing. They had sapped the kids' powers. How? He still didn't know quite how it had happened. He remembered thinking about how wonderful it would be if those brats didn't have powers, and figured he could use those fragments against them somehow, but he never expected that result.

He giggled, giddy with power. He had studied the group for months before he approached them, knew all their powers, knew how they had gotten them, learned as much of the Apa Tuni rituals as he could through his limited resources. The fragments must have picked up on that knowledge and used it somehow. Oh, who cared how it worked. No more would Morgan Taylor or Rilo's Runts be a threat to his would-be domination of Fairfield. He was king of the hill now. And he loved it.

Rilo and Norbu had passed him on the other side of the street and didn't even realize it. They were moving so fast, how could they? Racing to the brats' rescue no doubt. He had to laugh again. Life was just too good.

What he hadn't realized was that a dark, shadowy figure had been watching him from the rooftops.

The dark figure had deftly matched his prey's movements, leaping from rooftop to rooftop, easily keeping pace.

Preston stopped four streets up from the scene of the bus accident and ran into the middle of the road. He could see police lights, news crew vans, and fleeing citizens about another ten streets down.

Looking around cautiously, he placed the fragments on the ground and slid the manhole cover to the side.

He stepped onto the ladder, grabbed the fragments, then disappeared down the dark hole—heading for the spot where he and Kyle had come through the rip.

The darkness swallowed him. He and Kyle

had felt their way along before. Now, the fragments flared, glowing brighter, cutting through the gloom. This was definitely his best day. The slimy walls glistened in the green glow as he splashed through the ankle-deep water. He turned down a side passage, positive it was the route to the rip.

He was right.

The rip shimmered in the air, a crackling, twisting tear of white light.

He smiled and started forward.

Then, someone tapped him on the shoulder.

He turned and found himself staring at a dark, heaving chest. He looked up into the face of the Collector—and everything that was Preston Talmalker fled his mind in a painful instant.

The Collector had pushed into his consciousness with ease, taking control. Preston felt enormous pressure in his skull, like the worst headache he had ever had times a million. Tiny dots exploded before his eyes as his face beaded with sweat.

No longer in control of his body, he found himself raising his arms, opening his hands, and letting the fragments drop into the Collector's waiting claws.

With the prize in hand, the Collector turned, studying his latest acquisition—another piece to the puzzle. No mere contest. No simple prize. This was something special. He would discover its secret. And keep it for himself.

Preston dropped to his knees with a splash, gasping for breath. For some reason, his brain kept forgetting to tell his lungs to breathe. The spots exploding before his eyes grew larger by the moment, and his chest was an agony of stabbing pains.

The Collector tossed and turned the metal shards in his leather-gloved hands. Simply exquisite. Traces of light raced along the surfaces of the metal, into the crevices and grooves, like beads of luminescent water. He could almost identify some of the pieces. They were not random fragments at all, but sections of tiny gear-wheels, bolts, perhaps even a sliver of a control rod or two.

Interesting.

After all his years in the game, in all his vast collection of the bizarre, he had never seen anything quite like—

The memory hit him with the speed and

fury of a hurricane.

He remembered a workshop table in a darkened room, lit by the faint golden glow of a brass oil lamp. The wooden surface was covered with papers, diagrams, drawings of creatures, sketches of unfathomable monsters. Renderings of dreams—nightmares—as he recalled.

In his mind, he felt the excitement again as he held that diagram with human hands— twelve—or perhaps thirteen-year-old boy's hands.

The diagram was of an incredibly complex machine, much more complicated than any he had previously glimpsed in his short life.

He remembered the drawings hidden beneath it.

He knew better, he remembered thinking. A real sore spot—this item in particular. He remembered harsh words, "sticky fingers—whining voice—tired of you—taking what is not yours."

The tall shadow from behind.

The strong hand smacking the diagram away.

The strong hand striking his tender, tear-stained face for the first and last time.

He remembered a sorrowful embrace.
He remembered a fallen temple.
And a well.

Suddenly released from the choking mental grip, Preston rubbed his throat, sucked in breath after breath, then flung himself headfirst through the rip.

Something stirred inside the tall, reptilian form standing in the sewer. He looked up from the metal fragments.

He was no longer sure that he truly wanted this prize after all.

RAISING THE STAKES

After a mental message from the Game Master that the contest had ended, the weary contestants returned to the tavern where more than a few hostile words were exchanged with Guerendet.

"Ah, you can all go jump, ya whining babies," the rotund, owl-man retorted, waving off a crowd of angry hunters with his stubby hand.

Jerry sat at a corner table with the recovering Snod. The skinny nerd had his head tossed back and a cold compress applied to the back of his neck. His nose hadn't stopped bleeding since the earthquake he had inadvertently caused.

Snod had managed to re-form shortly after the quake subsided, much to Jerry's relief. It was an emotional reunion.

Preston Talmalker found himself backed

into a corner, literally. Kyle Banner thrust a finger into his chest, threatening to tear him limb from limb. Darren and Skinny Joe backed him up. They were all not so gently reminded that while in the tavern, everyone was protected. Preston declined more than one request to step outside.

Morgan, Frank, Hank, Shelly, David, and Michelle sat together, a group of wounded veterans, at a table near the wall of famed hunters. The highs of their heroic acts had long since faded.

"What are we going to do now?" Hank asked, playing with the Merely Magic Magic Wand® that he had managed to retrieve from the warehouse. "I mean, now that we can't change into anything any more."

Morgan didn't say anything.

"We're gonna die! That's what we're gonna do," Shelly proclaimed angrily.

"C'mon. What kind of talk is that? We're not gonna die," Michelle said. "David came without powers, right?"

"I had you guys to protect me before. Face it. We're dead," David groaned.

"I don't know—I think they're right. I

think we're gonna die," Morgan said, his voice trailing into space, his eyes wide with fear.

"What kind of thing is that for a leader to say?" Shelly asked. "You were supposed to disagree with us!"

The wand rose in Hank's hand again, poking through his closed fist like a rising antenna.

"Hank. For the love of everything that is just and fair in this forsaken world. Please—tell me how that thing works," Frank moaned, as he lay his weary head on his arm.

"No way," Hank said. "Then it wouldn't be magic." They both watched it rise again through his loosely clenched fist.

Morgan continued, gravely, "Rilo won't perform the Apa Tuni on us. I already asked. He's glad we're normal kids again, wants us to have a normal life. He thinks we can just lay low and live through this. Yeah, right. If we quit, we're dead. But if we play, *they* are going to *kill* us."

The kids looked at the throng of hunters and creatures around them. They all seemed to be staring in the kids' direction, with countless snarls, countless cracking knuckles, and countless ill wishes.

"Brrrrrrr," Shelly said.

"Yes," Frank replied dully. "We seem to be lacking in the well-wishers department."

At the table across from them, a group of hunters, Juskk, Deschaul, and the Valli sisters among them, were having a meeting of their own.

"We want them dead," Calle Valli said, twisting her long brown hair into knots. Her sister, Salle, allowed her fangs to extend to their full three-inch length, which was quite long for fangs. The sisters were wearing identical casual outfits, fashionable leather jackets, boots, black jeans, and sky blue T-shirts. Many mistakenly thought of them as vampires, though they were actually a less hairy, more attractive form of lycanthrope. The sisters, supernatural smugglers by trade, also dabbled in pirating and assassination.

"And dead they will be. Just leave it to me," Juskk croaked. "The moment the next contest has begun. I know where it's going to be held. Brakk is making arrangements." He didn't move his head at all when he spoke. His neat, brown beret didn't move an inch. His eyes couldn't be seen through his aviator-style goggles, but the white scarf partially covering his face had fallen slightly, revealing the greenish scar tissue hidden beneath.

Deschaul straightened in his seat and said, "I don't know about you, but as for myself, I plan on taking it easy this next leg. In fact, I shall scarcely hurry at all. I'm resigned to the fact that Anastasius will triumph—and I say fine. I feel rather foolish for joining this contest at all."

The others didn't say anything, but they could tell the feeling was fairly mutual, throughout the entire tavern.

Rilo and Norbu stood in front of the glass case that held the first two sets of metal fragments. The shards and pieces were arranged like a wreath, nestled inside a molded red-velvet-lined case. The lights traveling along the surface of the pieces were dazzling to behold.

The Game Master himself stood nearby, unwilling to wander too far from the case, but not getting too close either.

"<Did you notice?>" Norbu asked.

"<That he has no scent?>" Rilo replied, nodding toward the Game Master, who nodded in return.

"<He's unnatural. He scares me.>"

"<These things scare me more. How, Norbu?>" Rilo wanted to know. "<How will these

fragments help the tribe? How will they free the others? What did the Game Master mean? You escaped the slave camp, Norbu. Do you see any connection at all? Any possible use for these artifacts?>"

"<No. Not yet. We must continue to play as hard as we can. We need to secure the final pieces for ourselves. See if we can use them to gain the other fragments somehow, then figure out how everything works.>"

"<*If* what the Game Master said is true at all. We only have his word. Regardless, with the two of us together again, Orin Surr had better be trembling.>"

Norbu didn't say anything.

Rilo sensed a presence approaching from behind. He knew the scent immediately, but the cold chill gave the figure's identity away.

The Collector seemed to pay the Buru no mind as he gazed intently into the glass case, hands firmly behind his back.

"Nice isn't it, Collector? Too bad, you'll never see the other pieces until they're safely here in our claws," Norbu boasted.

"Do you know what they are, Anastasius?" Rilo asked, respectfully.

The Collector gazed down at the Buru.

"They are part of something that doesn't belong here. It doesn't belong anywhere. It's not a trinket, and it's not a prize . . . It should be destroyed."

Rilo didn't know exactly what the Collector meant, but he could tell the statement was heartfelt.

The Collector took a final look at the pieces, as if mentally assembling them. He then walked up to the Game Master—and brushed past him.

Rilo and Norbu rejoined the children from Fairfield, sitting down at their table. Kyle, Darren, and Skinny Joe finished threatening Preston in the corner and walked over as well.

"Well, the final round is going to start any second. Hope all your major medical is paid up," Darren joked.

"This isn't funny, Darren. We're really in trouble here," David told him.

"I think we should just take a cue from the rest of the crowd. I've heard everyone else is just gonna let the Collector have the last pieces. Not quit, you know. Just not try very hard to win. If we do the same, we should be okay," Skinny Joe said confidently.

"I can't do that, Joe," Rilo said. "I need those pieces. You know that. They could help free the other Buru."

"You don't need those things. You got us, remember?" Darren said.

Norbu groaned and slumped in his chair, his ears sagging.

"Look. I mean as soon as this thing is over—BOOM, baby. We're off to free your Buru buddies. Just like we promised," Darren replied, trying to be as 'up' as possible.

"Darren! You are not stupid! Quit *acting* stupid. You are a kid. Just a *little* kid. You don't *have* powers. You can't *wolf-out* anymore," David said sarcastically. "We can't help, here. It's not that we don't want to, but the fact remains— we're powerless. They'll kill us easily now. I'm with Skinny Joe, believe it or not. We lay low. We go home."

The others thought heavily about what the elder Donaldson had to say. Although his forecasts were usually grim, there was a ring of truth to what he was saying this time.

"What—What about what we did at the

bus?" Michelle said. "We made a difference. We saved those people—*without* powers."

David leaned forward. "There's a big difference between being brave and being stupid. Saving people who are in danger at the risk of life and limb is brave. Looking to attack the forces of the supernatural with nothing but charm and good looks? That's stupid." He tapped the table top for emphasis.

"As much as I hate to say it, David is right," Rilo agreed. "You should all lay low, let this contest end, then go home. Norbu and I will—"

"Oh, so that's it! Mr. My-Best-Buddy-Buru shows up and all of a sudden you don't *need* us pathetic humans any more. Oh, I needed you for a while, but I don't need you anymore, so now you can go home?" Morgan shouted in disbelief.

"That's not it at all, Morgan. You know that. How can I take you all to certain death? In a way, I suppose, it's *good* this happened. You're human again. *Truly* human."

Morgan was furious—to the point of tears. "This isn't about being human or being a Buru," he said, trembling. "It's about being friends."

Rilo sensed the rising emotions around the

table. He thought hard before continuing, trying to choose his words well. Feelings were not easy for a Buru to express, although at that moment, he was overcome by them.

"I thought I was giving you all a great gift when I performed the Apa Tuni ceremony—when I gave you powers. I thought I could be the great tribal leader of a great tribe. I was wrong. I can't lead you. I'm not qualified. You *are* a great tribe— of *humans,* not Buru. Though I see now that's what I wanted you to be. To be the family I missed so much. The family I couldn't save."

All eyes were on him now, and no one was saying a word.

"I have a precious chance to get back the family I lost," Rilo continued. "I don't want to lose another in the process."

The Game Master approached the center of the room.

The third round was about to begin.

STAMPEDE!

When the light faded and the rip closed, the kids found themselves falling into a sea of waist-deep yellow grass.

"OW!" Darren cried. "David, if you fall on me again, so help me—"

Morgan and Frank shot to their feet and immediately began scanning the vast field for signs of other drop-ins, knowing full well they couldn't afford a surprise. Not now.

"See anything?" Morgan asked.

"No," Frank replied. "I would guess we're on an African plain."

"Maybe we got lucky. Maybe no one landed anywhere near us."

At that moment, behind a dead tree a few feet away, Preston Talmalker fell through a rip in the air and landed unceremoniously on his head.

Kyle saw him, and smiled.

"Kyle, wait!" Morgan yelled. "He may have an artifact or a cursed seal on him or something. Stay away from him!"

Morgan's orders fell on deaf ears. Kyle saw Preston face down in the grass, and nothing was going to stop him.

Nothing except the thing that was coming up behind Preston. The sight of it made Kyle back away—slowly at first, but more quickly as full realization hit him.

The others first saw Kyle running back toward them, then saw what he was running from.

A hundred yards behind Preston Talmalker, the tall grass parted in an approaching wave, as if being flattened by a giant steamroller—a steamroller about fifty yards wide.

Even from that distance, they could hear the unmistakable, trumpeting cries, could feel the ground thunder beneath hundreds of galloping feet.

Hank's eyes shot open the widest—for he knew the trumpeting battle cry of the Nandi better than anyone.

"RUN, PRESTON!" Hank shouted, joining the others as they turned to flee across the plain.

Preston managed to haul himself to his

feet and groggily began running after the others.

The hideous black heads of the beasts burst through the grass first, their eyes glowing yellow, staring from under their long black hair. They tossed their massive heads as they ran, eager to impale anything in their path on their monstrous tri-horns.

"RUN! RUN, COWARDS!" Juskk cried, his muffled laugh carrying across the field. He was astride Brakk, who was leading the entire herd.

"WHAT'LL WE DO?" Shelly screamed.

"RUN! RUN FOR YOUR LIFE! THAT'S WHAT!" Michelle screamed back.

"FRANK! CAN HANK HELP?" Morgan gasped, running up beside the fleeing Dunks.

Frank realized what Morgan was asking, "HANK! CAN YOU SPEAK TO THEM? DO YOU REMEMBER THE LANGUAGE?"

"I GUESS SO," Hank huffed, struggling to keep up with the others. "WHY?"

"TELL THEM TO STOP, YOU IDIOT!" David yelled.

"FRANK!" Hank gasped.

"APOLOGIZE, DONALDSON!" Frank snarled.

"I'M SORRY, HANK! I JUST DON'T WANT

TO DIE!" David cried, nearly catching up with Skinny Joe, who was the still the fastest of them all.

Darren made the mistake of looking back over his shoulder. He gasped as he saw the grass falling beneath the wall of stampeding Nandi. Preston was only a few feet in front of them now. Their great, hippo-like mouths opened and closed, eager to taste the fleeing boy.

"PRESTON'S HISTORY!" Darren shouted.

Morgan looked back and saw just how true Darren's pronouncement was. He turned and ran back toward the enraged Nandi!

"IS HE CRAZY!" Shelly yelled.

Morgan pounded back through the grass, the approaching wall of galloping doom coming up way too fast. He could see the absolute terror in Preston's eyes.

"NOW! HANK! TRY IT NOW!" Morgan shouted, he and Preston a heartbeat away from crushing death.

Hank stopped, cupped his hands, and let loose with a barrage of unintelligible grunts, gronks, and trumpets. The sound carried over the field with astounding strength and clarity.

The Nandi shook their heads and, despite the best efforts of Juskk, splintered off in all directions, running randomly—all one hundred and fifty of them.

Morgan leaped, hitting Preston low, knocking him from the path of a charging Nandi that was right behind them.

They rolled to a stop on the flattened grass and covered their heads, the beasts running all around and past them.

Brakk, too, fell victim to Hank's command, charging off, with a furious Juskk struggling for control.

Michelle, Shelly, Joe, and the others fell to their knees, straining for breath, as if they'd just run the hundred-yard dash.

As they caught their breath, they began to laugh, each patting the amazing and masterful Hank Dunk on the back.

"Well said, Hank. Well said," Frank sighed in relief, as proud as was humanly possible of his little brother.

Farther out in the field, Preston and Morgan sat up.

"Oh, man," Preston gasped. "You—You saved my life! Can—Can I rejoin your team?"

At that instant, Morgan Taylor punched Preston Talmalker hard in the mouth.

REUNION

Rilo and Norbu stood up and shook their heads, still feeling the effects of the rip.

When Rilo looked around, he saw that they were standing at the point where a sea of yellow grass met a vast forest. A light breeze rustled the treetops outlined against a warm blue sky.

Under any other circumstances, it would have been an astoundingly beautiful place to be on a perfect day.

"<There!>" Norbu said, raising his long striped arm, pointing toward the forest.

Rilo saw what he was referring to—a white stone building, ancient and crumbling, covered with leaves, dirt, and vines. It reminded Rilo of a beehive. It was shaped like a squat, ribbed bullet, with large stone columns and numerous branch-covered walkways made of buried stone blocks. In fact, Rilo noticed, buried square stones extended far into the forest, winding snakelike in all directions. Around the temple, in geometric formations, various trailers and semi-trucks formed a high-tech human settlement. Rilo could hear the generators and see the strings of electric lights running from wire suspended high in the trees.

"<Where are we? What is that place?>" Rilo barked.

"<I—I can't believe it,>" Norbu gasped, swelling with excitement. "<Look! There's your answer!>"

Rilo looked again toward the strange complex and thought his heart would stop.

Another Buru.

He was small, grayish green, and carrying a small metal crate toward the temple's front entrance. Rilo could scarcely believe it, but it was true. It was real. There was another Buru, stopping in the middle of that walkway, dropping his crate, stretching his back and ears. Rilo saw still another marching down the steps of one of the trailers, toting a similar box. His pulse raced. His breathing grew shallow and for a moment, he thought he would faint. A million thoughts crashed through his mind at once, a lifetime of memories in the Buru village in the Himalayan valley. Sights, smells, feelings he had long forgotten and that only a Buru would know. He watched a small pack of his kind, talking excitedly, rushing along the sidewalk toward the temple.

His kind.

Rilo watched in awe, a mist of tears momentarily clouding his vision. His mouth turned up in a grin, and he wanted to say something to Norbu, but found he had no words—none that could properly express what he was feeling.

Rilo nearly cried, realizing fully that he was not the last Buru.

"<The final leg of the contest. Here! Here of all places! In the slave camp of Orin Surr! Incredible!>" Norbu barked. "<Fate has truly delivered us, my friend! This is most fortunate!>" His ears shot up, and his delight changed to alarm. "<DOWN! Quickly!>"

They ducked into the tall grass as a gray-skinned, wrinkly man in a tan uniform marched by. He was holding a rifle of an unfamiliar, high-tech design. The man had thin wisps of black hair that hung from his wrinkly head, no nose to speak of, and large mounds of vein-covered skin stacked in bunches around his neck. A Goula, notorious guards for the slaver Orin Surr, renowned in supernatural circles as the most dangerous and merciless of all mercenaries. The man-creature peered into the grass—sure he had heard something stirring inside, sure he smelled fear.

Rilo and Norbu didn't move a muscle or draw a breath. They were as still as two statues, fear raging like fire through their brains, both fighting their instincts to attack while the element of surprise was theirs.

After what felt like an eternity, the Goula moved on.

"<Who was that?>" Rilo whispered.

"<A Goula, one of Orin Surr's mercenaries and researchers—very good at what they do, exacting, obedient, and cruel. They constructed the complex around the temple—designed their weapons. Their technological skill is matched only by their arrogance and utter lack of regard for other life forms,>" Norbu whispered. "<And they despise Buru in particular.>"

Rilo spotted several more Goula, walking along the rooftops of the trailers and around the temple's columns. Then, he spotted the more familiar form of the dog-like Barghest, chatting with several of the Goula, also brandishing high-tech rifles.

"<Follow my lead,>" Norbu said, stepping from the grass when the coast was clear. He marched toward the temple with his hands held together in front of him, his head bowed.

Rilo did the same, walking beside him.

They strode right past several passing Goula who didn't give them another glance—that is after Norbu dutifully chirped and nodded toward them.

In fact, Rilo and Norbu nervously walked through an entire army of Goula, reaching the temple entrance without inciting a single shout of alarm and without a single one of the hundreds of rifles being raised. They looked at each other as they mounted the steps and sighed in relief.

Walking inside, Rilo immediately sensed that a great restoration was going on, and the Buru slaves were the primary labor.

The room was vast, round, and seemed endlessly tall, curving upward to a point. Dark, twisted vines snaked from every crevice and corner, hanging like tangled nets on the walls. Tree limbs and clear sky could be seen through several holes in the ceiling. Rilo noted dozens of passageways leading from the center chamber, lit by flickering yellow lights. He suspected the passages led to other chambers, deep underground.

They made their way around and under the various platforms and scaffolding that towered above them, occupied by Buru slaves who busily restored the walls with carved white stones and mud.

Norbu motioned him toward one Buru in particular. The Buru was busily restoring a faded mural, a muted rendering inside an indentation on the wall near a side passage entrance.

Teebu was very engrossed in his work, applying colors with an artist's flair. He closed one eye, cocked his flat, reptilian head to the side, then worked on another spot. The mural depicted a strange, glowing figure stepping from a well. The figure brandished a shimmering sword and a small cylindrical object.

"<You missed a spot,>" a raspy voice said from behind.

"<What? Oh! Thank you, I . . . >" When Teebu turned around, his ears stood straight up and his mouth opened wide in surprise.

"<RILO! Can it be possible? Is it really you?>" He grabbed his long-lost friend by the shoulders and pulled him close, holding him tightly.

"<Easy, easy, Teebu. We can't draw too much attention,>" Norbu cautioned.

"<My friend, I cannot tell you how joyous this is for all the Buru. We feared you were dead! Killed by the Collector.>"

"<It's a long story. I'll tell you, later—as soon as we get you all out of here.>"

Teebu shook his head. "<Even the mighty Truro slayer couldn't manage a trick like that. Someone else will be happy to see you alive, friend. CUKO!>" Teebu yelled.

A short, blue-green Buru looked down from a scaffolding high above their heads. He leaped to the floor with graceful ease.

Cuko straightened, took one look at the Buru who was standing with Teebu, and nearly exploded with excitement—which captured the attention of the Goula guards.

"<RILO!>" Cuko exclaimed. "<I can't believe it!>" He grabbed his friend and held him tightly. "<We thought you were dead! Is it really you? Ha, HA! When the others hear, they'll be . . . >"

"<It's great to see you, too, Cuko.>" Rilo said, clutching the Buru's arms. "<There is so much I want to ask. So much I've missed. Is Kala here? Nodu? Is Rina all right?>"

"<There will be time later, Rilo—after more pressing matters,>" Norbu said, lowering his voice as another Goula took notice of their unauthorized congregation.

"<Of course. You're right,>" Rilo said. "<Old times can wait—until after the escape.>" Rilo's confidence was growing by the moment. His eyes glowed brightly, his small form barely containing the energy radiating from within. Simply being near his old friends made him feel unstoppable—invincible.

"<Escape?>" Cuko asked, unsure if Rilo realized what—

"Escape is something that will elude you, Buru," a voice boomed from the door.

Rilo turned to see a fat Goula in a stained, white undershirt standing in the doorway. A bandanna was wrapped tightly around his greasy, wrinkly gray head, wisps of black hair hanging down the sides. A pair of mirrored glasses sat on the small bump in the middle of his face.

"Orin Surr, I presume?" Rilo asked.

Orin seemed surprised.

"You know humanspeak? Impressive, swamp-dweller. Now why don't you come with me quietly—so we can talk privately."

The Buru on all the various platforms stopped their work and looked at their enslaver, and the source of his irritation. They saw Rilo and could scarcely believe it. Norbu had succeeded, they thought. He had actually brought Rilo the Truro slayer back.

Rilo sized the Goula up, narrowing his glowing red eyes, baring his sharp teeth. "Why don't you spare yourself a whole world of grief and let us go—Now."

A small squad of Goula and Barghests crowded in around their leader.

"Somehow, I don't think the boss would like that very much," Orin growled. "Not when he's this close."

"Close to what?" Rilo asked.

"Close?" another voice rang out, approaching from behind the squat form of Orin Surr. "Why, close to bringing my quest to a successful conclusion, of course."

Rilo felt an intense rage course through him as Orin stepped aside and he saw the identity of the speaker.

The Game Master.

"Welcome, Rilo the Buru. I would say congratulations—but you are by no means the first to arrive."

"Why, slaver? Why did you bring me here?" Rilo growled.

"Egotistical little fellow, aren't you?" the Game Master said. "Your attendance here is necessary, but undesired."

The Goula soldiers and the Barghests raised their rifles and drew nearer.

Teebu and Cuko backed away, trying to blend in with the other Buru as they watched, growing sick with dread anticipation.

"Would it surprise you to know that it isn't you I'm after at all?" the mysterious figure said.

Not me? Then who? Rilo thought, then realized the meaning of the words.

"NO! They're only children."

"Children who've managed to defeat, outwit, or outshine nearly every hunter in the circle. Not a small feat, for anyone, child or hunter alike."

"Why would you want them now? They're powerless—merely human," Rilo snarled, backing up to Norbu, preparing to fight as the Goula and the Barghest soldiers drew closer, surrounding them both.

The Game Master strode past Orin and glared at Rilo and his stalwart friend. The Buru's comments had filled the tall, mysterious man with rage—though he managed a controlled, venom-filled response.

"Now, there you go again. Merely human? You underestimate your own team, Buru? Amazing. Despite your less than adequate training, the children prove themselves formidable again and again, and still you doubt them. You truly puzzle me, Buru. You held those who could possibly be the strongest in our circles. Yet you wished to trade them for these—these reptile servants? A foolish bargain, I would think." His voice seemed to fill with delight as each word stabbed Rilo's heart. "The children are no longer your concern. I will teach them, guide them to their true potential—as only a human could do."

Those words hit Rilo like a sledgehammer. For a moment, he saw Morgan at the table. Saw the boy's rage at the Buru's own careless words.

The Game Master continued. "My best agent will take great care in delivering them to me—in a performance to be long remembered."

The guards drew closer.

"<You will not touch them, slaver. We will die first! Ready, Norbu?>" Rilo asked.

"<Yes,>" Norbu said. "<I'm ready.>"

Rilo watched Norbu walk away. Watched him walk over and take his place beside the Game Master and Orin Surr. His friend since they had been nestlings. His unwavering ally through difficult hunts and long wars. His dream-trader and faith-lifter. Norbu. His best friend. "NORBU!" he shrieked, loud enough to shake the room.

Norbu said nothing, looking away as the guards descended on Rilo.

The other Buru, gathered all around the room, witnessed every blow, every kick, but felt powerless to interfere. The Goula rifles would cut them in two if they so much as moved. They had learned that bloody lesson in a swift, costly, and decisive rebellion a very long time ago. A rebellion Norbu had led. Teebu placed a claw on Cuko's shoulder and nearly cried.

Though Rilo fought hard and well, his mind—dulled by shock, coping with treachery, and clouded by anger—conspired against him, and he fell to the butt of a rifle.

A SECOND CEREMONY

The children had been crossing the grassy plain at a rather leisurely pace for an hour or so, not anxious to run into other contestants. In fact, they hadn't seen any one else as they headed toward the forest on the edge of the grassy plain.

"MORGAN! COME QUICKLY! HURRY!" Hank yelled.

Morgan plowed through the grass, rushing toward Hank, who was standing over something, pointing down excitedly.

Hank had wandered off and was slightly ahead of the rest of the group when he'd made his discovery.

Morgan and the others reached Hank and saw Norbu lying on the ground breathing heavily.

"He just burst through the grass and fell down!" Hank cried. "Is he all right?"

Morgan leaned over to help Norbu as the Buru struggled back to his feet.

"Morgan. We have trouble. It's the Buru! Orin Surr's slave camp is in the woods—not more than a mile or so from here!" Norbu gasped.

"What?" Morgan cried.

"The third part of the contest is in the slave camp?" Frank asked.

Norbu nodded, still out of breath.

"Where's Rilo? What happened to Rilo?" Morgan asked.

"He was captured. We were surrounded by Orin Surr's dog-headed soldiers and Goula guards. We fought bravely but there were too many of them. I barely escaped! You have to help me free Rilo and the others! Please. I—need your help."

"*Now* he needs us," Skinny Joe said.

Morgan didn't say anything though he shared Skinny Joe's opinion. He didn't really like Norbu very much—nor trust him. Still, Rilo was in trouble.

"What can we do? We have no powers, now. They'll annihilate us," Darren said.

"We can't just let Rilo die, can we?" Michelle asked.

"We have to do something!" Shelly exclaimed.

"If we just march in there, we'll get slaughtered," Kyle said.

Morgan thought and thought, pacing back and forth, trying to put the pieces together in his head.

"Morgan," Frank said. "This is too strange. Why would the contest just happen to take place at the Buru camp? Why are there no other contestants around besides the one who set the Nandi on us? It's as if they were nowhere around here—placed far enough out to not interfere."

"Interfere with what?" Morgan asked.

"Us. It's as if we were *supposed* to be the only ones left. It almost seems to be—"

"A trap?" Morgan finished.

They both looked at the Buru, doubled over, struggling for breath.

Suddenly, Skinny Joe exploded with excitement. "I'VE GOT IT!" he yelled. He consulted with Darren who quickly agreed, nodding his head.

"Norbu!" Skinny Joe asked. "Can you perform the Apa Tuni ceremony on us? Give us our powers back?"

"WHOA!" Shelly cried.

"YES! THAT'S IT!" Michelle agreed.

Everyone looked to the brownish, striped Buru with great hope—even Frank.

Norbu shook his head. "I—I don't know how. Rilo studied with the mystics of the Apa Tuni tribe. They showed him how. Only he knows how to do it."

Frank and Morgan looked at each other, unsure of what to do next.

"It's up to you, Morgan," Frank said.

Morgan stepped forward, hesitating before he spoke.

"I—I can do it."

"What?" they all asked incredulously.

Morgan spoke with a shaky voice. A scared voice. "I can perform the ceremony."

"Yeah, right," Kyle scoffed.

"Impossible," Shelly agreed.

Darren and David didn't quite know what to make of the bold statement.

Michelle, Frank, and Hank walked up to Morgan—believing in him completely.

"Really, Morgan?" asked Darren.

"Really. I think I can do it. I've been studying it. I'll try—but only if we all agree."

The kids exchanged questioning glances, until finally all eyes turned to David. David had never gone through the ceremony. Denied it. Steadfastedly refusing powers, desiring only a normal life free from the weirdness that seemed to plague them all.

"Well?" Morgan asked again.

"What do you say, David?" Darren asked his brother.

David thought about it for what seemed like an eternity before saying—

"For Rilo's sake. Okay."

The children all gathered around Morgan. He closed his eyes, thinking of all he had learned, concentrating. His body began to tremble, and his hands rose high above his head, as he began to recite the words to himself—powerful words uttered outside the Apa Tuni village only one time before.

The air grew charged and heavy just as it would have right before an impending thunderstorm.

With each word, crackles of light danced around them. Dark clouds formed in the sky, churning and boiling.

In the center of it all, the small boy became a conduit of immense power.

Darren was the first to feel it.

He grabbed his head, wailing in pain.

He doubled over, surrounded by a greenish glow. His ears seemed to grow long, as did his fingers. Fangs grew from his mouth, sharper than before. Thick, black hair sprouted across his hunching back. *Darren felt himself become the Werewolf again—but this time he was different. Stronger. Faster—more dangerous.*

Kyle's arms grew long and hairy, more powerful than before. He felt his brow furrow, two puffy leathery sacks swelling, enclosing his face. His teeth became razor sharp, and he grew seven feet tall. *Kyle looked around through the eyes of the ape-like Pendek.*

Frank's skin turned orange and scaled. His body elongated into a thick coil, and his neck widened into a massive hood. His tongue forked as *Frank again became the towering snake.*

Feathers sprouted from Michelle's skin, completely covering her body. Gigantic wings grew from her back as her hands and feet changed into huge claws with deadly talons. *Michelle* soared into the air, the proud thunderbird.

Shelly's face flattened as her body bulked and fur completely covered her. She flexed her toes, springing her claws as *Shelly the phantom panther.*

David felt his flesh thicken, becoming a thick scaled hide. His eyes bugged into glassy orbs as *David turned into a fearsome lizard-man.*

Skinny Joe's body sprouted black fur, as a snout emerged from his face and his eyes glowed red. His thick, massive body dropping to the ground on all fours, *Joe had become the ghostly black-hound.*

Hank felt extremely heavy as his mass increased forty times in a blink of an eye. Ropy thick fur hung from his monstrous body as he roared his approval. *Hank was again the lumbering Nandi.*

Morgan was last. He felt an odd tingling, the sensation of growing new limbs—wings, green and bat-like, spreading from his shoulders. But he was different from last time—stronger. Larger. A whip-like tail, tipped with spikes, swished through the air behind him. His head stretched and sprouted fins. His nose lengthened, becoming a snout. *Morgan felt himself become a humanoid dragon.*

Each child, in turn, became a beast, a crea-ture after his or her own heart. Together they stood around Morgan the Dragonoid, their undis-puted leader, no longer human children, but a strange force all their own.

Then, as swiftly as the power had come, it left them in a great flash, a wave of light travel-ing upward.

They regarded each other a moment, grow-ing used to their new appearances, their new powers, both familiar and unfamiliar at the same time.

The Dragonoid spread his wings and growled. "As Darren would say, let's go kick some monster tail."

Norbu smiled.

A LESSON
IN DECEPTION

Rilo's cage was barely big enough for him to turn around in, about four-feet square. The sides were dented metal, flaked with rust. The smell convinced him it had been used many times. Before losing interest in thoughts of escape, he had peered through a small opening, seen the other cages, and realized that his was not unique. They all had electronically controlled locks, metal pins for stackability, and front gates cut with long rounded slits, as if somehow the lack of bars would make it less a prison.

The room that housed the cages was extremely dark, lit only by the eerie red glow of the power units below the grated floor. Large pipes ran the length of the room, overhead and from floor to ceiling. He could smell unfamiliar, noxious chemicals flowing through them into ceiling-held storage tanks. What he guessed to be medical life support stations and computer-controlled monitors were built into rolling metal carts placed around open cages and near glass-walled cubicles.

Judging by the rectangular shape of the room, and the steady patrol of marching feet pounding on the roof, Rilo guessed he was in one of the trailers outside the temple.

When the door at the opposite end of the room opened, daylight poured in, proving him correct. He held a trembling claw to his face, blocking the blinding light from his eyes. A silhouetted figure climbed the last metal step, walked in, and closed the door behind him, returning Rilo to his gloom. Rilo listened to the hollow metallic echo of footsteps as they approached and recognized the gait.

When Rilo lowered his claw, he found himself staring into the somber, striped face of Norbu. The treacherous Buru searched for words that weren't easily found.

"<They're coming for you in a few moments, and I wanted to say goodbye,>" Norbu barked.

"<To kill me, I suppose,>" Rilo said.

"<No. To change you. The dig at the well level is extremely dangerous. Hidden pockets of poison gas. Unstable shelves of rock. The work is impossibly difficult. In the beginning, we dropped like flies, maybe a dozen a day or more. The Goula found a way to alter the Buru's structure, making them more resilient for the work. Unfortunately, it—well, you'll discover for yourself soon enough. Though they've found the final fragments, Orin feels it would be worthwhile to continue the dig. There may be other artifacts of power still to be found.>"

Rilo shifted, his red eyes the only thing Norbu could see through the shadows.

"<Well—Aren't you even going to ask why?>" Norbu said.

"<No. What does it matter now?>" Rilo replied, the red glow in the cage vanishing as he closed his eyes.

"<Oh—I see,>" Norbu growled angrily. "<Poor Rilo. Failed to save his tribe from destruction so many years ago. Failed to mold his new tribe into the powerful force it could be . . . Now, he has failed them for the last time.>"

Rilo didn't say anything.

"<You don't realize it, my friend, but you

have saved your people. You will be remembered as a hero of the highest order. You have offered up a grand sacrifice—a trade. The freedom of those human children for the freedom of the Buru.>"

Rilo roared, his claws struggling to lash out between the slots of the cage. "<I've offered up nothing! This was by your arrangement! What did he tell you, Norbu? Will it be as simple as that? You believe that you and the others will simply walk out of here?>"

"<Yes.>"

"<You're a fool, Norbu.>"

"<A fool who was has delivered freedom to the others—something I knew you could not do. Not with your sick, sad, misplaced loyalty to the human children.>"

"<Norbu, what have you done? Look what you've done to me! Look what you've done to them! You've destroyed their lives.>"

"<Their lives are just beginning—in the service of the Master. They are here already. I led them to the temple. They are sweeping the restoration rooms and the dig in the lower levels, searching for you. The master is quite ready for them.>"

"<They'll never join him.>"

"<Then they will die . . . I've never under-stood your devotion to the humans, Rilo. Not with the Apa Tuni in the old days, and not with these children now. Of all the creatures in the world, of all the wondrous species and entities in all of the circles, you ally with humans above all, even your own. Have you no pride in your heritage? Have you no regard for what it means to be a Buru? With the contest, you chose to help your human friends before fighting for your own? WHY?>"

"<I'm not sure I understood myself, Norbu, but you have shown me. Morgan was right. It isn't about being a Buru or being a human . . . It's about being a friend.>"

"<You chose the wrong friends.>"

Rilo stared at Norbu. "<I chose one wrong friend.>"

The door opened again, and three Goula guards walked in, brandishing rifles.

Rilo felt a lump rise in his throat as they approached. He didn't care about himself, but his one regret was that he could not save his friends, Buru and human alike, from certain treacherous doom.

"<He is ready,>" Norbu chirped, as he walked by the guards.

They grabbed Norbu's arms.

"<What? What are—>" Norbu cried, struggling as they dragged him backwards.

He cried out in pain as they twisted his arms and flung him into the cage beside Rilo's. They swiftly locked the front gate, flipping a series of tiny, glowing switches.

"<NO!>" Norbu cried.

"<What was that again about choosing the wrong friends?>" Rilo asked.

TO RESCUE THE BURU

The sudden altercation between Teebu and the guard had drawn a small crowd of both Buru and Goula. Shouts of anger and alarm reverberated in the vast room, part of the primary dig site. The room was cavernous, with carved stone walls blending into natural rock facing. As in the temple, many scaffoldings, wooden support columns, and metal platforms served as restoration workstations for the Buru slaves. The sheer size of the project demonstrated the Game Master's desire to restore the age-old temple to its former glory.

Now, the Goula raised their rifles, aimed, and prepared to end the dispute before it got out of hand.

Cuko pushed through the crowd. "<TEEBU!>" he cried.

229

Teebu had made the mistake of striking a Goula guard, though he couldn't have helped himself. Now, a deep, running gash split the angry guard's many chins. The gray, wrinkly lump of a man had demanded that Teebu work faster, then went on to laugh with another guard about what would happen to Rilo and Norbu, how stupid and vain the Buru were as a species, and how glad he would be when Orin would see fit to get rid of them all. The other Buru had suspected Norbu's treachery when he had first vanished from the workplace, and rumors of Rilo began sweeping the Goula ranks. Teebu, like the others, had hoped Norbu had indeed brought Rilo to help in the fight for their freedom and, like the others, felt all hope dwindle when Rilo fell and Norbu revealed his own blind, self-destructive nature. The guard's remark had proved to be the final straw.

As the other Buru listened to the hum of the laser rifles, their growing anger began to overtake their fear.

"Kill him. Kill the worthless reptile," one of the guards shouted.

"<NO!>" Cuko shouted, his eyes glowing fiercely, his claws growing long. A rifle butt slammed the back of his head and sent him sprawling onto the floor of the cavern.

"Hey! Yeah you! Elephant man! Pick on someone your own size," a powerful voice rang out from above.

The crowd, Buru and Goula alike, looked up to see a Dragon-boy hovering beneath the cracked, domed ceiling. His green, scaly wings stirred the air with each flap. A pointed tongue snaked out of his pointed snout. His eyes, cracking with electrical blue fire, flared to blinding white.

In a green blur, he swooped into the surrounding Goula, twirling like a tornado. Each guard dropped his gun with a yelp, finding his hands had been sliced by the creature's whirling claw-tipped wings.

A guard on a high scaffolding raised his rifle, ready to fire at the Dragonoid, but a large furry claw wrapped around the barrel and plucked it from his grasp. The guard found himself staring into the snarling, terrifying face of a black Werewolf. "Play nice," Darren growled, then punched the guard in the face, sending him plummeting over the edge of the scaffolding to the floor below.

Three Barghests raced along a catwalk near

the center of the crumbling stone ceiling, taking positions to fire down into the gathered Buru. They raised their rifles—failing to see the large, golden eagle soaring in behind them like a jet-fighter. They howled as Michelle the Thunderbird's wings knocked them head-over-heels in passing.

"JOE! Do you see Rilo or Norbu any-where?" Michelle cried.

A Black-Hound with glowing red eyes bound-ed through a crowd of Goula, effortlessly avoiding their clutches. "NO! I don't see them!"

After ducking for safety, Teebu rose to his feet, looking around the chaotic room and mar-veling at the monstrous children wreaking havoc on the Barghests and the Goula. A giant orange snake had coiled around a support column, crush-ing it as if it were paper, sending a platform full of thugs to the floor. A large hairy Nandi charged a rushing crowd of Barghests, sending them flying through the air. A lizard-man stepped from the wall in a shimmer of light, where he had blended in seamlessly a moment before, punching two Goula from behind with powerful claws. A mon-strous Pendek strode past Teebu, twirling a Goula guard over his head like a fan, then flinging him into a rushing squad of Barghests.

"<Rilo chose his new tribe well,>" Cuko said, his voice hopeful.

"<Yes. But there are too many for them,>" Teebu said.

Their conversation was cut short by the sudden bump of two large, dark legs from behind. They turned to find themselves staring up at the Game Master.

He scarcely seemed to notice them as he regarded the scene around him, then laughed long and hard.

"HOLD!" he shouted, with a voice loud enough to crumble the ceiling. His voice had a clear, resonant quality that demanded both attention and reverence. It was as if his voice were the only sound in the chaotic room.

Everyone in the room stopped fighting and stared at the dark figure, his head completely covered by a skintight, black hood, no eyes, no nose, no mouth—only a black void where a face should have been. He was wearing a jumpsuit similar to the Collector's, but darker, seemingly as empty as his featureless face.

"Dragonoid," the Game Master said calmly, soothingly. "Today, I offer your brave team a chance. A chance to save yourselves. A chance to save your Buru friends. A chance to save your former mentor. And a chance to grow more powerful than you ever dreamed possible."

Morgan landed and folded his wings. One by one the other children gathered around him, all eyes on their dark host.

"Together, you have faced obstacles and nightmares that have destroyed others—flourished and thrived where many others have failed. This contest served many purposes for me. Among them, the chance to judge your team. To see if you possess what I require. I offer you the chance to be a force for me. A truly remarkable force, capable of learning what I have to teach, of adapting and growing in a world of astounding new possibilities—a world greater than your wildest imagining."

Morgan didn't say a word.

Teebu, Cuko, and the others felt devastating fear tearing at their hearts—fear for the lives of the human children.

"The Buru can teach you nothing else," the Game Master said sincerely. "*I* am your next step. Your logical progression. I offer you your greatest adventure. I offer you nothing less than a new world."

The kids looked all around as the Game Master raised a hand and a hundred more Goula and Barghest soldiers filled every doorway and passageway. The yellow lights of their rifles glowed in the dust-choked gloom.

The Buru slaves found themselves thrust toward the center of the room, pushed forward by both hairy and wrinkly hands.

"Accept, and Rilo and the others will go free. You have my word. Refuse, and they all die. Choose. Time is short."

The kids, dumbfounded, looked at each other, each contemplating the offer the Game Master proposed.

Morgan stood with his large, scaly fists clenched, his fiery blue eyes locked on the blank void of the Game Master's face.

Morgan could sense the soldiers raising their rifles, training them on the small group.

The dark figure stepped forward without a sound and extended a black-gloved hand. "Do you accept?"

Morgan looked at his teammates, into their eyes.

He knew the answer, as they all did.

For Rilo's sake.

THE GAME MASTER REVEALED

Rilo could still see Norbu, or his cage anyway, not that he really wanted to. The Goula technicians rolled his cage into one of the glass cubicle rooms, then rolled one of the metal tables continuing the medical equipment within easy arm's reach. They placed strange masks over their mouths and eyes.

Norbu started to scream before they even began doing anything. The glass window clouded over completely from the fumes of noxious chemicals as the technician tested the instruments.

"I can manage this one. You start the other," the guard said with the disinterest of someone who had performed this procedure far too many times.

Rilo saw the gray man coming for him, strolling casually.

"All righty then—Ready, pal?"

The Goula wasn't paying attention. His mind was somewhere else, on other things, perhaps what he was going to do later that evening.

It was all the opening Rilo needed.

The Goula found himself lifting his arm without really wanting to, watching it as though it were someone else's appendage. It took a moment for Rilo to root through the muck in the gray man's brain, but he found the code that would release the lock, forced the man's fingers to replay it, clumsily but effective enough.

The lights on the lock danced.

The lock opened with a sigh.

The Goula saw a blurry streak, caught a glimpse of a coiled, scaly fist, and felt the hard metal grate on the back of his head as he hit the floor—then blackness.

Rilo bounded down the metal stairs at the foot of the trailer and ran into the main yard. The temple loomed ahead of him. He looked all around, on the defensive, scanning the now-empty stone sidewalks and trailers for attackers. There was no one around. Then, he heard the commotion coming from inside the temple. Felt the ground beneath him rumble.

"The kids," he said, his alarm and fear growing.

He ran as fast as he could, his speed approaching seventy miles an hour as he soared past the towering trees and columns, flying through the temple entryway.

Rilo used his every sense, some long dormant, straining to pick the children out from every other presence in the temple. Those senses led him down a dark, winding maze of passageways, to a round hole cut in a cavernous wall. Four Barghests stared anxiously through the hole at something happening far below.

Rilo took them down with three well-placed kicks and dropped onto the uppermost scaffolding of the main hall.

Far below, he saw the Game Master facing the children. The children were in creature form—but different.

"Morgan. You did it," Rilo muttered, scarcely able to believe his eyes. Despite his alarm and concern for their immediate safety, he felt a glow of pride.

Rilo had made it just in time to hear the

Game Master's offer.

He, like the other Buru, the Goula, and Barghests, waited anxiously for the answer.

Morgan the Dragonoid smiled, looking up into that black, expressionless face that towered above him and said—

"The answer—is no."

Teebu cheered, yelling at the top of his voice, followed by Cuko and then the rest of the Buru tribe.

The Game Master stepped back, the room growing darker as he screamed, "DESTROY THEM!"

The kids all closed their eyes and concentrated. A reddish glow mushroomed from their bodies, encasing them in a crackling red dome of energy.

A hundred volleys of laser fire erupted from rifles all around the room at once, striking the dome—bouncing back to their sources.

The surprised Barghests and Goula howled and screamed as their ranks were caught in rounds of their own fire, falling from scaffoldings and platforms alike.

The dome dropped, and the kids and the

Buru fought hard, side by side, attacking all within reach.

The strange force of monstrous children and Buru worked together fluidly, making mistakes, but quickly covering for each other—taking down wave after wave of attackers. Miraculously surviving in the face of impossible odds.

For a moment, Rilo thought of jumping into the fray and aiding his friends, but as he watched them fight, he thought better of it. Morgan was arcing the room in great sweeps, drawing the soldiers' fire into each other. Joe and Shelly were attacking small squads together, high and low. Kyle, Darren, and David plowed through hordes of Goula, their desperate blows never missing. This was a different team, Rilo thought. They had never fought like this before, had never displayed such skill, such combined purpose. He saw then what the Game Master saw in them. Saw what he hadn't seen before.

Rilo smiled and decided that, for the moment, they didn't need his help at all.

He had another destination in mind.

A place picked from the mind of the Goula technician as he had so graciously opened Rilo's cage.

The lowest level in the temple.

And a well.

The Collector stared down at the gathered pieces glittering with traces of light and, for the first time in a long time, found himself undecided.

The room was incredibly dark, except for the orange light flickering in the hallway and the streaks of yellow racing along the surface of the fragments. When he had arrived and infiltrated the room, he had found all the fragments gathered together, in a case similar to the one at the tavern.

The fact that the fragments were there waiting for him wasn't a surprise at all. It took a fool not to realize that the Game Master, who gathered and contained the shards after each contest, wanted the pieces for himself. That they served a purpose of his own design. The fragments' function still eluded the Collector—though he had a fairly good idea. The machine that would be created from the fragments was incredibly intricate and complex—circular in shape, like a ring.

A ring that would fit the indentation on the crumbling stone well quite nicely.

The well sat in the center of the room, surrounded by columns that towered into the darkness, joining high overhead in great arches.

The Collector looked to the far wall of the cavern and saw the abandoned picks and electric cutting tools lying on the ground, no doubt abandoned in the excitement of the discovery of the final shards. The generators sat silent, the floodlights off.

He looked at the faded murals on the walls, painted eons ago. They depicted glowing beings, standing in suns, extending to the tribesmen blackened articles cut with complex lines. They were neither the first, he thought—nor were they the last to cross over to this world.

The Collector cautiously picked up the case of fragments and carried it to the indentation at the base of the well.

He moved cautiously because he knew that he was not alone—though his keen senses couldn't pinpoint the mysterious onlooker's position.

The Collector placed a small flashlight in his reptilian mouth and swiftly went about his work.

His thickly scaled fingers moved swiftly, his mind constructing and reconstructing the mechanism a thousand times over, directing and redirecting his hands. The task didn't take long, scarcely under three minutes—though it would have taken others far, far longer.

When the last piece was in place, the ring flared with a brilliant glow, the lights racing along its surface in great streams.

It was a Ceques, the Collector decided.

A Ceques like no other. And like the original, it had *not* come from this world.

For a moment, he recalled a night in 1806, over two hundred years earlier, when he, his brother, and their guests from the manor fought an intruder the likes of which the world had never before known. The otherworldly creature stormed through a rip in the air onto the outlying fields of Fairchild Manor. Again, he felt the sheer terror that the monster had inspired, just as his brother's nightmare drawings and designs had terrified him when they were younger. He had found himself struggling furiously at the glowing opening, clutching the alien's weapon. Had felt the creature's cold hand on his own. Had felt its life ebb away as he turned the strange blade against its owner.

The Collector held the device for a moment

and felt the enormous power it contained. Already it seemed to be directing him, delving into his mind, attempting to reconstruct what it found there into something more to its liking. Were he human, it would have taken control instantly. But now his defenses were stronger, and it struggled with him.

It was wasting its time, he thought, in the command it repeated over and over.

He had every intention of doing exactly what it wanted.

He placed the mechanism into the indentation on the well.

Rilo arrived in time to see the Collector bend over and put something down.

Then, the room exploded, rocking and crumbling in a flash of blinding white.

Rilo found himself blown into the hallway in a cloud of stone debris. Coughing and shaken, he climbed to his feet, then stared into what was left of the room.

He saw that most of the columns around the well had fallen, though a few had remained upright—barely. The mural walls were clawed and scarred, half buried behind fallen stones and jagged rock.

The well in the center of the room erupted with geyser after geyser of swirling greenish mist, periodically bursting with sprays of bluish light.

Then, he saw the Collector lying on the ground and about forty feet from the well. His helmet had fallen from his head, his black coat was torn, and he wasn't moving.

Quickly, Rilo bounded across the fallen stones and rubble, fearing the ceiling would come crashing down.

It was then that he peered into the churning emerald pool, and saw something that made his heart jump.

In the distance, beyond the misty opening, lay a shimmering city, bathed in vermilion light. The city from his dream. It was the city out of which the Buru had come to greet him. And it was at that moment Rilo knew what must be done.

He bounded over to the Collector's fallen form.

"Anastasius," he croaked.

The Collector rolled over and glared through weakened, snake-slit eyes. One had turned red with blood.

"We've been had, Buru," the Collector whispered, the calm in his voice unnerving the little reptile.

"What do you mean? The device—what is it doing?"

The Collector continued, ignoring the Buru's question. Rilo was not sure if the Collector even realized he was there.

"Why—" the Collector rasped. "Why did the hideous creatures ever find us—discover us? Why do they not stop meddling in our affairs? Cursing us—"

"Who? I don't understand?"

"Foolish, Buru. You were to give him an army, I was to give him the key. Of the two of us, it is unfortunate—that I succeeded."

"What are you talking about. The key. The key to what?"

"The key to the other world. The source of all things supernatural. He wants to go there as he always has. Explore the amazing realm. He threatened to take us both there, more times than I care to remember. I knew he would never let it go. Never stop trying."

"Who? Anastasius? WHO?"

"My brother."

Rilo felt a presence then. A cold, ghastly presence he had not felt before. It was walking toward them both.

Rilo shot to his feet and whirled around to see the Game Master effortlessly gliding across the debris. His strides were unfaltering, even as the room shook under the blast of another geyser from the well.

"Anastasius. I knew you would succeed, dear brother. I had every confidence. You always were the plucky one."

"Langdon," the Collector growled, struggling to his feet.

Rilo backed away as the two dark figures regarded each other. They stood before each other in mirror-like fashion. Their posture, their stature, their manner—nearly the same. They could have been twins—if Langdon's hidden face were also reptilian.

"No hug?" Langdon asked.

"I killed you once," the Collector said with a low snarl that chilled Rilo to the bone.

"Yes. Yes, you did. But I forgive you little brother. You have opened the door for me, and for that I'll be eternally grateful. I'd have done it myself, but it would have proven quite fatal. I have an—oh—aversion, to that little mechanism now. Like you, it wants back what it gives. However, I've grown rather attached to my life. Think I would miss it."

The geyser from the well erupted again, licking the roof with a long green tongue of flame and mist.

"You may thank Rem Tullock and his sentimental burial arrangements for my return, Anastasius. It was rather fortunate that he and I grew so close. I knew you would not honor my burial wishes, but he took great care to see that I got what I wanted. It was one of the devices he buried me with, this device, that allowed me to return to life! It opened the door to the other world and let me wander inside! And then it shattered, sending me back to this miserable rock and scattering itself all over as well. I searched for the pieces, and when I found some of them, I was horrified to learn that they had become poison to me. Coming into physical contact with them would kill me! So once I located all the pieces, I formulated the game, and chose my pawn."

The Collector seethed—and placed his hands behind his back, silently undoing a metal clasp on a compartment of his belt.

Langdon wagged his finger in the air. "Ah, ah, ah. No tricks, Anastasius. I've waited FAR too long for this moment. AND YOU, BURU!" Langdon cried.

"I am VERY disappointed in your little team. They chose not to go with me! Most ridiculous—and booorrring. I was actually rather surprised. Children usually have such a marvelous sense of adventure about them, such a refreshing lack of fear of the unknown," Langdon said, staring at the Collector. "Well—most do anyway."

"We do not belong there, Langdon—as *they* do not belong here."

Suddenly, the Collector's hands flew from around his back, as fast as lightning.

A black bolo finished its final pass—harmlessly—around Langdon's forearm.

Langdon lowered his arm and said, "I'll say hello to our good friends for you—if they've forgiven us for your rude behavior in that field so many years ago."

The Collector backed away. Though emotionless on the outside, inside he was erupting like a volcano. Rilo drew closer to him, unwilling to simply run.

"Enough of this." Langdon turned his head

toward the well, watching the bluish lights that streamed up from its depths. "Come, little brother. You should go also."

The Collector stood next to Rilo and spoke clearly and confidently to his brother, for what Rilo guessed to be the first time.

"I am not going, Langdon."

Langdon seemed hurt, the remark cutting him deeply. "Then I offer both of you a going away present."

A white, ragged, nightmarish form emerged from behind Langdon. Its pebbled skin was ashen gray, flecked with white, as if it had been dipped in flour. Its eyes were like two clouded marbles, and its jaws quivered, opening and closing involuntarily.

Langdon cried with insane fury at his younger brother. "DEATH! At the hands of the one you enslaved!" he then turned to Rilo, "—and the one you adored!"

Rilo choked.

It was Norbu.

PROTECTING THE FAMILY

Rilo stared at his former friend and realized there was nothing left of Norbu in that horrific shell.

It lurched forward like a starving animal, drooling from the mouth. Its claws rhythmically curled open and closed. There was to be no reasoning with it, no subduing it. It would kill him either with its vicious claws or with a well-placed bite.

The Collector stared into the Norbu-creature's eyes and saw nothing there. No sentience at all. Only a drone with a single programmed thought.

Kill.

The white monstrosity leaped, and Rilo moved to intercept it. They met in the air and rolled to the ground, Rilo desperately countering

251

each frenzied blow. The creature's jaws, lined with razor sharp teeth, snapped at his arms, tearing large gashes, trying to sink into his throat.

The Collector used Rilo's attack to dodge away from Norbu's assault. With an angry roar he lunged into Langdon, knocking them over a pile of stone rubble near the well.

The greenish glow from the eruptions made them appear as two silhouettes locked in desperate combat.

"Norbu," Rilo wheezed. "You have to fight it. FIGHT IT!"

The wild-eyed monster locked its ashen claws around Rilo's neck and squeezed and squeezed—choking the life from the flailing reptile.

The light in Rilo's eyes began to fade, growing darker and darker as Norbu laughed and laughed. It was an idiot's laugh, an insane laugh that comes from an unthinking entity— giddy with satisfaction that its programming was being fulfilled. Its claws tightened, its arms shook, its laughter erupted in great whooping howls.

Rilo thrashed and thrashed in its grip, pulling, scratching, and kicking his predator in the belly with his claws, but to no avail.

Rilo's eyes grew dimmer and dimmer.

Then, with a rustle of breath and a slight shudder, the light died completely.

The soft, green creature in Norbu's claws went limp. The monstrosity grunted, deeply satisfied, then let the form fall from its ponderous arms like a wet sack.

Langdon gouged at the Collector's face with his hand, pushing into his brother's eyes with his fingers.

Wracked with pain, the Collector roared and lost his grip on his brother's collar, but managed to shove him away.

Langdon staggered back and felt the stone surface of the rim of the well beneath his hand as he struggled to keep his footing.

He looked down into the well as another geyser of green light erupted, knocking him and the Collector to the cavern floor.

The white, heaving Norbu-thing hovered over the body of its kill, tendrils of drool pooling on the lifeless green chest.

It turned heavily, searching the darkness for the other for which it had been programmed.

Rilo's eyes flickered very faintly. He had to be sure the creature was not paying any attention to him as he made the call.

Morgan the Dragonoid was busily breathing a cone of fire at the support ropes of a Barghest-filled scaffold when he heard the call. Its suddenness and urgency startled him, breaking his concentration.

"Rilo!" he cried, hearing the faint message inside his head. It was Rilo, there was no doubt. He struggled to hear what his Buru friend was trying to tell him.

The scaffolding fell, accompanied by the screams of half a dozen Barghests.

"Teebu!" Morgan cried, not really knowing whom he was yelling for, only that Rilo wanted someone called Teebu.

Below him, in the thick of the battle, a rather heavy Buru stopped and looked up at him. "Are you Teebu?" Morgan yelled.

The Buru nodded, barely dodging a charging Nandi trying to shake four Goula from its snout.

"Rilo wants you to get to the well. You are to bring the others. He says you're all going someplace far away. Someplace safe. Somewhere he knows you'll be free!"

Teebu nodded, signaling Cuko, who, after taking a few rifles from the Goula, was fighting with the aid of several of his Buru friends, firing volley after volley into the charging Barghest thugs.

"<Cuko! Get the others! We're going to sanctuary!>" Teebu cried.

"Darren!" Morgan cried.

The black Werewolf jumped from platform to platform, avoiding angry Goula soldiers, until he was at eye level with the flying Dragonoid. "You rang?"

"Rilo's okay!" Morgan cried. "He's all right! We have to keep these creeps busy for a few more minutes until the Buru can get out of here! They're heading for another level! Get everyone to cover them!"

"No problemo!" Darren the Werewolf snarled, leaping back to the floor.

In a matter of moments, the monster children stepped up their defenses. They managed to keep the remaining soldiers from interfering with the steady stream of fleeing Buru as they flew into the tunnels.

The entire temple shook, sending cascades of rock and dust down from the ceiling, as the eruptions from the well grew larger and more violent. Bits of stone broke away from the well walls as shafts of blue light shot through the sides.

The Collector, sprawled on a cluster of shark stones near the well, turned to his side and touched his head. Blood.

Langdon sprang to his feet and stepped up onto the well wall. A towering green geyser exploded up and around him, making him cackle with manic glee.

"Goodbye, my brother. Hope to see you on the other side someday!" He turned to step into the well.

The Collector lunged through the air and tackled Langdon, knocking him clear of the well, smashing into one of the only standing columns. The stone cracked against the impact of their tumbling bodies, and they both cried out in pain.

Norbu started toward the stunned dark figures lying on the ground by the columns, but was startled by the appearance of more Buru, two of which were familiar somehow.

Teebu and Cuko, leading the other Buru,

stopped upon seeing the transformed Norbu, absolutely terrified.

The more Norbu stared, the more the familiarity didn't matter. Only the pain in his head mattered, and the burning desire in his pounding heart. The desire to kill. He growled, baring his fangs, ready to tear into the lot of them.

He didn't see the green form rise up behind him—clutching a big, square stone.

When the stone crashed down on the back of his head, he became furious beyond measure. His clouded, milky eyes opened wide and rolled back in his powdery white head. He felt himself reel on his feet, but immediately began to shake off the effects.

Rilo didn't waste a second, he tore into the Norbu-thing again, punching and kicking with as much devastating accuracy as he could deliver. Each claw and bite would have brought down any other Buru, but not the hideous monster he was facing.

"<GO!>" Rilo yelled. "<IT'S SAFE, I SWEAR TO YOU! GO NOW!"

Teebu and Cuko, having complete faith in their legendary hunter, led the others quickly, stopping at the rim of the well.

Then—one by one—the Buru jumped inside.

With each jump, the geysers flared, like splashes from a pond, the air rippling with bluish light.

"<GO! HURRY!>" Teebu cried to the others, watching Rilo as he struggled valiantly with the transformed Norbu.

They rolled and wrestled, kicked and clawed, tearing at each other with intense savagery. Never had Teebu seen such battle. Never had he seen someone fight so hard for the sake of others. Teebu watched as Rilo stood down the only beast nastier than the great Truro—and realized he was watching a legend in the making.

Cuko tugged his arm frantically, indicating that they were the last ones to go. Teebu nodded, sending Cuko through first.

Teebu caught Rilo's eyes, just before he jumped. He didn't see pain, though he was sure there was plenty, didn't see worry, or remorse, or even anger.

He saw joy. And in Teebu's head, he heard Rilo say, "Good luck, my friends."

He nodded and smiled in reply—then jumped.

"NOOO!" Langdon cried, struggling with the Collector, furious that the lowly Buru—not he, but the lowly Buru—were the first through the great door to the other world. The sheer injustice of the situation made him snap—for an instant he lost his concentration.

And that was all the Collector needed.

Langdon heard something whistling through the air as he turned back to his brother.

He caught a coiled, scaly fist square in the face, sending him flying through the air to land ten feet from the well—in front of Rilo and the Norbu-thing.

The Collector hadn't quite had the time to regain his composure when the well exploded with the largest eruption yet, shaking the temple at its very foundations.

The walls of the cavern shook and crumbled, dropping sheets of rock to the floor with a huge crash.

In the temple's main hall, the remaining Barghests and Goula fled, running as fast they could to escape the temple before it collapsed.

"MORGAN!" Frank the Snake yelled. "I believe these moronic goons have the right idea!

Leaving would seem very logical at this point!" The scaffoldings had all but fallen, their narrow metal floors dangling from snapping ropes. "Any word from Rilo?"

"No!" Morgan the Dragonoid cried. "Quick! Who's got the Ceques piece?"

"I DO!" Hank the Nandi roared. He bounced the piece off the tip of his horn, up to the Dragonoid's clutching hand.

"You guys get out of the temple! I'll grab Rilo and meet you!"

"BUT—"

"Just go! There's no time to discuss this as a committee!"

With that, the Dragonoid soared into the underground passages.

Rilo lost his grip, flipped onto his back, and stared up into the flashing fangs of death that raced toward his throat.

Then, a flying black bolo bounced off the Norbu-thing's head, nearly breaking its neck, buying the moment of distraction Rilo so desperately needed.

"The mechanism, Buru. Destroy it. NOW!" The Collector yelled. Langdon screamed and tackled him from behind, sending them both flying into the sole remaining support column.

The ceiling began to fall in huge, jagged chunks. One piece, as large as a piano, landed with a crash beside the Norbu-thing, knocking him farther off balance.

Rilo bolted to the indentation in the well that held the mechanism as another geyser tore through the ceiling, bringing a rain of debris down upon his head.

"Smash the device! Seal the door! DO IT NOW, BURU! WHILE THERE'S TIME!" the Collector demanded.

Langdon gripped his hands into one fist, swung with the force of a wrecking ball and connected with the Collector's chin. The reptile-man stumbled back, nearly leaving the ground, falling into the darkness toward the rear wall.

Rilo mounted the wall and looked down into the well. He stared into the swirling green mist—*saw another world*. A new world. A strange world. Yet one that felt safe and familiar.

His tribe was there.

There, they would be safe.

Langdon, the Collector, and Norbu circled each other in the dark. The world was caving in around them, but they didn't seem to notice or care.

"DO IT, BURU!" the Collector yelled.

Rilo jumped down from the wall.

He picked up a large rock.

The device in the indentation exploded into a million glittering fragments as the rock connected, driven home with all the force the small Buru could muster.

Rilo heard Langdon's scream of anguished protest and Norbu's deafening roar as the ceiling toward the rear of the room collapsed, sealing the three of them off, burying them behind tons of rubble.

The rooms above were collapsing on the rooms below, and Rilo realized there was nothing he could do to save himself. He looked up and waited for the sky to fall.

"RILO!" Morgan the Dragonoid cried, zooming through the entryway, crashing through the waterfalls of rock at incredible speed. He sailed into the Buru, grabbing him around the waist while cutting the very fabric of the air with the Ceques sliver.

They both vanished in a blinding white light as the temple collapsed completely.

PICTURE WORTHY

It was snowing hard again.

The kids and a handful of others were the only ones left in the Salem Queen. The temperature had dropped to zero outside, and the fire in the large stone hearth was comforting, indeed.

Morgan had dispatched the bruised-jawed Preston, using the Ceques sliver to send him back to his large home in Mullenfield. The conniving little creep swore vengeance on the kids. Kyle said, "Goodie."

The other contestants, incensed at being placed so far from the prize in the final round, went home disgruntled and bitter, but already talking about a future tournament.

Only Snod, Jerry, Guerendet, and Vicade remained, and would remain—until Guerendet was allowed to win at least *one* game of cards.

Shelly, Michelle, Skinny Joe, and Darren were grilling David about how it felt to have powers, what they were like, did he feel any different as a lizard-man? He responded by seeming to vanish into thin air, reappearing with a ripple, his camouflage ability in high gear. He and Darren shook hands, equal partners at last.

Frank followed Hank to the bar. Hank had promised that if Frank could talk the tavern keeper into making them all milkshakes, he would be inclined to show Frank how the magic wand trick worked.

Rilo stood in front of the empty glass case that used to contained the fragments. The round indentation was bare, the red velvet cloth gleamed in the small spotlight. His mind wasn't really on the mechanism, or the contest, or even the kids. He was smiling to himself, relishing his short but priceless visit with Teebu, Cuko—and poor Norbu. He could practically see the others, in the fields and valleys of the other world, building a new village at the base of a mountain, in a nice cozy swamp. Rebuilding the great tribe of which Rilo was so very proud to be a part. Almost as proud as belonging to his *new* tribe. His *human* tribe.

"So how does it feel?" Morgan asked.

"Hmm?" Rilo said, startled from his waking dream. "Sorry. How does what feel?"

"How does it feel to be the last Buru?" Morgan joked.

Rilo smiled, looking fondly at his best friend, placing his claw on his shoulder.

"I'm not."

As Hank picked up their milkshakes, and Frank excitedly and repeatedly performed the magic wand trick, he asked the tavern keeper if she would be so kind as to do one more favor—

Later, as the janitor mopped the floor around the tables, the tavern keeper carefully hung and straightened the latest picture on the wall of heroes.

It was a picture of Rilo the Buru—one of the best people you'd ever meet.

About the Authors

Marty M. Engle and **Johnny Ray Barnes Jr.**, graduates of the Art Institute of Atlanta, are the creators, writers, designers and illustrators of the **Strange Matter™** series and the **Strange Matter™ World Wide Web page.**

Their interests and expertise range from state of the art 3-D computer graphics and interactive multi-media, to books and scripts (television and motion picture).

Marty lives in San Diego, California with his wife Jana and twin daughters Lindsey and Haley.

Johnny Ray also lives in San Diego, California and spends every free moment with his wife, Meredith.

STRANGE FORCES

FORCES

Creature Files

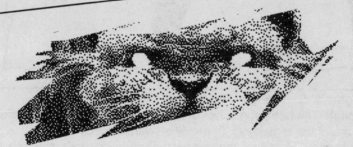

A close-up look at
some of the strange creatures
and monsters that inhabit
the world of
Strange Matter.™

BURU

Height: 3'-5' **Weight**: 60-100 lbs
Habitat: The farthest reaches of Northeastern India, in a lost valley at the rim of the Himalayas. Primarily a swamp-dweller.
Attributes: Reptilian, the red-eyed Buru is an agile creature with sharp claws on its hands and feet. Fast as a cheetah, they can reach speeds up to 70 mph. Highly intelligent and verbal.
History: The Buru have long been a common neighbor to the Himalayan Indian tribes, most notably the Apa Tuni. Carved wooden statues, stories, and songs portray the Buru as figures of fear and superstition—creatures with strange powers. The Buru, in turn, have little to do with humans, preferring to keep to themselves, allowing for little interactivity between their tribe and the Apa Tuni. *Except Rilo.*

Rilo Buru studied the Apa Tuni, their rituals and their way of life, their language and their magic. He believes himself to be the only survivor of the day of the great, black cloud—*the Collector's gathering.*

THE COLLECTOR

Height: 6'2"   **Weight**: 225 lbs

Attributes: With a wide variety of supernatural artifacts at his disposal, the Collector's powers are immense and ever-changing. He possesses the power of telepathy and immense physical strength. Equipped with the skills of a master hunter, he is a practically unbeatable opponent—even without the help of his army of monsters.

History: Founders of Fairfield in the early 1800s, Anastasius and Langdon Fairchild, were inventors and explorers. When a creature from another dimension ripped through the fabric of time and space, invaded their town, and was killed, the brothers discovered that the alien had brought two items with it—a magical sword, and a supernatural map called the Ceques. Langdon hid and studied these items until his mysterious death years later. Anastasius continued to study the power of the Ceques—*and vanished*!

Anastasius became a treasure hunter, acquiring unnatural artifacts and unexplained creatures. He amassed an amazing collection—leading to the name he soon became known by within his circle of fellow hunters—the Collector. However, the magical items he gathered began to change his appearance—turning him into a snake-like creature. Now he uses the power of his artifacts and his monster army to build the greatest supernatural collection in all the world, *no matter what the cost.*

THE GAME MASTER

Height: 6'2"   **Weight**: 220 lbs.

Attributes: The Game Master is feared by most hunters, though few have encountered him. Stories of his ruthlessness and cunning are known worldwide. His strength is well beyond that of a normal human, and he possesses a unique rapport with creatures of the supernatural. He is able to calculate incredible odds and structure events to work in his favor.

History: The Game Master's past is shrouded in mystery. his name only a whispered rumor in the supernatural circles. Stories abound of this figure who needs no army, and who lays waste to his enemies with the help of his own macabre, supernatural inventions. His very presence creates disquiet in even the most notorious of figures, !ike the Collector and Rem Tullock. For the time being, lack of reliable information about his past and his methods works to his advantage. Though it is almost certain he has been involved with many unexplained phenomena, at present, no one can predict the motives of this mystery man or where he will strike next.

CREATURE FILE: NORBU

Height: 4'3"   **Weight**: 90 lbs

Habitat: The farthest reaches of Northeastern India, in a lost valley at the rim of the Himalayas. Primarily a swamp-dweller. Until recently, Norbu was held captive with the rest of the Buru in a stronghold somewhere in Africa.

Attributes: The Buru is an agile, reptilian creature with sharp claws on its hands and feet. Fast as a cheetah, they can reach speeds up to 70 mph. Highly intelligent and verbal. Unlike Rilo, Norbu's hide is slightly brown and has tiger-like stripes.

History: Norbu and Rilo were best friends before the Buru were separated. In fact, together, they faced the Truro, a creature that terrorized the Buru village. In the conflict, Norbu was almost killed by the vicious beast. Rilo defeated the Truro, saving Norbu's life. The rest of the Buru hailed Rilo as their greatest hunter, which may have sparked some jealousy in Norbu. However, they remained close until the Collector attacked and destroyed the village, capturing Rilo as a slave for his forces.

CREATURE FILE: REM TULLOCK

Height: 6'0"   **Weight**: 190 lbs.

Attributes: Of all the known hunters, Rem is probably the most experienced at his profession. Though he carries himself in a gentlemanly manner, one can see the battle scars, particularly a marble-sized, metal sphere which replaced his left eye. Rem is wise, careful, and does not draw attention onto himself. His skills in diplomacy and espionage, coupled with his superior tracking ability, make him a formidable opponent. His daughter, Amali, is his reluctant assistant and hunting partner.

History: Rem is over three-hundred years old. He came across his first supernatural artifacts while exploring the wreck of a pirate ship, accidentally bringing it's dead crew to life. After escaping that horrible affair, he studied archeology, and the burgeoning science of cryptozoology, before starting out on his own in search of forgotten treasures. His exploits brought him to Fairfield in the early 1800s, where he became fast friends with the town's founders, Anastasius and Langdon Fairchild. He stayed for a while, witnessing the Fairchilds' horrific encounter with a unknown creature from beyond.

    Rem has built his own supernatural empire, but kept an ever-watchful eye on the being calling himself, The Collector.

CREATURE FILE: AMALI

Height: 5'7"   **Weight**: 115 lbs

Attributes: When under stress, Amali's chalk-white skin becomes scaled and reptilian. Her eyes, black until facing a confrontation, glow bright-red. She has the strength of three men, and can run at speeds of up to forty miles per hour. Amali also has the ability to communicate telepathically. She is highly intelligent and is a superb hunter.

History: Amali was raised in the inner circle of supernatural treasure hunters. Her father, a renowned plunderer, claimed many wonders during his exploits—and exposed her to many of them. Over time, Amali developed certain powers of her own, over which she at first had no control. As her father's standing rose among his peers, Amali learned to master her abilities, and became her father's chief aide. During this time she met many powerful figures and experienced events far beyond fantastic. However, she recognized that these things are dark in nature. Her devotion to this darkness is constantly tested, but Amali will follow her father's orders—*for now.*

CREATURE FILE: GUERENDET

Height: 4'10" **Weight**: 220 lbs.

Attributes: Guerendet has an unnatural knack for controlling ectoplasmic beings: ghosts, phantoms, poltergeists, etc. Though they do not necessarily obey his commands, he can influence their actions and reactions, leading to many of their captures . . . and sales. His eyes grow to absurd proportions while searching for supernatural beings, and his features become owl-like. His strength and hearing are greater than a normal human's.

History: Guerendet's toughness and directness have helped him create a thriving supernatural trading business. When contracted, his army of employees scour the globe for desired creatures and items, stopping at nothing for a successful retrieval. They rarely fail, as they know failure means "termination" in more ways than one. He has a wicked sense of humor and enjoys causing chaos and catastrophes. His current favorite right-hand "men" are Snod and Jerry, whom he regards as moronic but effective.

CREATURE FILE: SNOD

Height: 6'5"   **Weight**: 300 lbs.

Attributes: Snod's skin is yellow-green and covered in large, runny zits. A thick, infectious fluid constantly runs from his nose and mouth. He communicates via a stream of gurgles unintelligible to anyone except his partner, Jerry. Underneath his slimy hide, Snod possesses thick, protective quills that spring out whenever he wants.

History: The underworld thug who would become known as Snod, once served as bodyguard to one of the most powerful supernatural leaders in North America. When his boss mysteriously disappeared, Snod—the ever-faithful servant—searched the country for his missing employer. His investigation led him to New York and the mysterious Rem Tullock, another well-known supernatural collector. During the ensuing struggle, a vile of powerful ectoplasm was accidentally broken at his feet, transforming him into a screaming flesh-bubbling monster. He met his partner and best friend, Jerry, while on an explosive mission for his current boss, Guerendet.

JERRY

Height: 5'11" **Weight**: 125 lbs.

Attributes: Jerry (last name unknown) has the ability (and the dreadful desire) to cause disastrously bad luck for anyone he wishes, ranging from spilling a drink to crashing a plane. He hasn't completely mastered his power yet and sometimes finds himself caught in the situation he created. That's where his second ability comes in handy. He is nearly indestructible.

History: Jerry had no idea he was a supernatural creature. He unhappily went about his life as a white-collar New York cubicle dweller. He regarded the astonishingly bad luck that plagued his coworkers and friends as simply coincidence . . . until, on one particularly bad day, he *consciously* caused a helicopter to smash through his floor of the office complex. He was the only person to emerge unharmed. After walking through a subway explosion (while straightening his tie and adjusting his glasses), he encountered the man-thing who set the bomb and found a life-long friend—Snod. He was offered a chance to use his unique abilities in the employment of the gloriously greedy Guerendet.

VICADE

Height: 7'11'   **Weight**: 340 lbs.

Attributes: Vicade can mesmerize an unsuspecting or unprotected human with his dazzling smile and soothing voice, bending them to his will. He is incredibly powerful, with strength matching a Pendek's. He can appear perfectly human at will and can generate fire with a thought. Though physically powerful, he is extremely sensitive, weak-willed, and a sore-loser.

History: Vicade rose to the most powerful ranks of supernatural collecting by lying, manipulating, and destroying anyone in his way . . . all with a dazzling smile and a friendly pat on the back. His expensive series of motivational tapes and videos, coupled with his mesmerizing ability, have given him the financial resources to scour the darkest corners of the Earth for supernatural artifacts. He is extremely neat and orderly, and tolerates no one's opinion but his own. The only thing he fears is losing his power, the only thing he loves is himself.

JUSSK & BRAKK

Height: 5'11"   **Weight**: 190 lbs.

Attributes: Jussk is a master hunter and smuggler. Hideously disfigured in a Nandi stampede, he wears customized, multi-viewing mode goggles and a thick scarf to cover his scars. He has tremendous underworld connections, is very good with technical weaponry, and can get anything in to or out of anyplace on Earth.

History: Jussk was once, among other things, an ivory hunter, tracker, and smuggler, tracking elephants to claim their valuable tusks. On one of these expeditions, Jussk fell victim to a Nandi stampede. He would have died if not for the intervention of Brakk, one of the largest Nandi of the herd. Brakk helped Jussk escape from the rampaging animals, and took him to a nearby village where he healed for many months. After recovering, Jussk urged the villagers, who were extremely familiar with the Nandi, to teach him about the magnificent creatures. Soon, Jussk and Brakk had developed a close rapport, and soon became partners in Jussk's dangerous and often unsavory exploits.

CREATURE FILE: GOULA

Height: 6'-8'   **Weight**: 225-300 lbs
Habitat: Anywhere, preferring residences in human settlements.
Attributes: These grey, bloated biped creatures possess great strength and technical prowess. Their skin is wrinkly and tough, with stringy black hair surrounding the crown of the head. They are good soldiers and able engineers, capable of constructing complicated structures, such as hi-tech lasers and mobile laboratories.
History: Pockets of these slug-like men have been found all over the world, but they seem to reside mostly in the middle-east and Africa. They often serve powerful masters as scientists and soldiers, and have average to above average human intelligence.